The TRIMONI TWINS and the CHANGING COIN

By the same author

The Last Burp of Mac McGerp

The TRIMONI TWINS

and the CHANGING COIN

PAM SMALLCOMB

BLOOMSBURY

First published in Great Britain in 2005 by Bloomsbury Publishing Plc
38 Soho Square, London, W1D 3HB

First published in the US in 2004 by Bloomsbury Publishing

A CIP catalogue record of this book is available from the British Library

ISBN 0 7475 7623 8
ISBN-13 9780747576235

All papers used by Bloomsbury Publishing are natural, recyclable products
made from wood grown in well-managed forests. The manufacturing processes
conform to the environmental regulations of the country of origin.

Typeset by Dorchester Typesetting Group Ltd
Printed in Great Britain by Clays Ltd, St Ives Plc

1 3 5 7 9 10 8 6 4 2

www.bloomsbury.com

To Victoria, Julie and my loyal writer pals, with thanks
And as always, to Rick

CHAPTER ONE

Great Cardini's knuckle hair!" said Beezel. She barely missed stepping on a five-foot-long boa constrictor as it wound its way across the room. "Mimi, can't you put your snake in the bathtub?"

Beezel sat down on the sofa, carefully moving a tarantula onto the floor before she did. "And can't you keep this spider in her cage?"

Sometimes Beezel's sister, Mimi, drove her nuts. They were going to be staying at the hotel for only two weeks. Did she have to bring every animal she owned?

"Gadget needs her exercise," Mimi said, scooping up the furry spider and putting her in a small metal cage on the end table. "I can't keep her locked up all day. And I can't put Gumdrop in the bathtub." She reached down, picked up the big snake and draped it around her shoulders. "I put my white rabbit in there. You know he and Gumdrop don't get along. Rabbits and snakes just don't mix."

Mimi opened up Gumdrop's carrier. It was a special portable habitat that the twins' father had made for the snake. "In you go. It's nice and warm inside." She gently rubbed the top of her boa constrictor's head. "She has a little bit of a cold, poor sweetie. She needs to get lots of rest." Gumdrop slithered inside. Mimi closed the top and looked at Beezel. "What time is the show tonight? Do we have time to get a pizza?"

"That depends," Beezel said as she straightened the books on the coffee table. "Did you do your homework? Did you practice the Amazing Levitating Snake trick? Because the last time you only got Gumdrop's head off the ground." Most of the time, Beezel didn't mind being in charge, but sometimes she wished Mimi would take a turn.

"Look," said Mimi, "just because Mom and Dad aren't here doesn't mean you can boss me around. We *are* the same age, remember."

"Actually," said Beezel, "I'm seven minutes older

than you. You're eleven years old. I'm eleven years old *plus* seven minutes."

"Big deal," said Mimi. "Seven minutes doesn't mean anything onstage."

Beezel and Mimi were magicians. Identical twin sister magicians. They came from a long line of circus performers. Their parents owned the Trimoni Circus, a small circus that traveled from town to town.

Both of the twins had raven-black hair like their mother, the Fantastic Flying Frederica; and both had turquoise blue eyes like their father, Eric the Eager Ember Eater.

But Mimi wore her hair short, cut straight across at chin level. She thought it made her look more like an artist. Beezel had decided that she was never going to cut her hair. It was much more practical to wear it in a braid down her back.

"Anyway," Mimi said. "Why do we have to practice so much? Why can't we just have some *fun* for a change?"

"Because it's opening night," said Beezel. "We have to do a great job. If we get good reviews, it will help Mom and Dad."

The Trimoni Circus had fallen on hard times. Some of their best acts had retired, and some had been lured away by other circuses with better pay. So a few years ago, Mr. and Mrs. Trimoni had decided to spend two weeks every fall scouting for new talent. While they were away, the members of the Trimoni Circus rested in a farmer's field in Baraboo, Wisconsin.

This year before her parents left on their search, Beezel found herself and Mimi a job performing magic in Baltimore, Maryland. The job description in the *Magic Monthly* was perfect. It had said, "Wanted: magic act for two weeks, at highly regarded small magic club, room and board included." The dates listed in the ad matched her parents' trip exactly.

Mrs. Trimoni had protested at first, but Beezel was determined. "The publicity will help the circus, and the money won't hurt either," she argued.

But Mr. Trimoni wasn't convinced. "You girls aren't going anywhere without a chaperone!" he said.

Wasting no time, the girls asked Mr. Whaffle, who taught the children in the Trimoni Circus. But Mr.

Whaffle was more than a teacher to Beezel and Mimi. He was like a member of their family.

Once Mr. Whaffle agreed to care for the girls while they were in Baltimore, Mr. and Mrs. Trimoni allowed them to go.

Mr. Whaffle had booked them two rooms at the Destiny Inn on Caroline Street. Beezel liked the sound of that: the Destiny Inn. Maybe it was a good omen—that they would do well and help the circus get back on its feet.

On the ground floor of the hotel was the Sleight of Hand Magic Club. For the two weeks that their parents were gone, the twins would perform there.

Beezel picked up a photograph of her parents from the end table. Mr. and Mrs. Trimoni smiled happily back at her from the rosewood frame. Mimi grabbed her backpack and plopped down next to her on the sofa. She leaned her head against Beezel's shoulder and stared at the photo.

"Where do you think they went this time?" she said.

"I don't know for sure," Beezel said. "They wouldn't tell me." Only Mr. Whaffle, and Hector, who ran the midway at the circus, knew how to reach them. "Dad was worried that someone would find out and grab the act before he could."

Beezel took a tissue out of a box on the coffee table. She polished the glass in the frame. "But I heard him talking about Tibet more than once. And he said something about finding a 'yeti' to Mom when they thought I wasn't listening."

Mimi's eyes widened. "Mom and Dad are after the Abominable Snowman?"

"I think so," Beezel said, laughing.

"I hope they packed warm clothes," said Mimi.

"And a big net." Beezel blew some tissue dust off the frame and set it back on the end table.

"Well, I wish I could have gone," Mimi sighed wistfully. She opened her backpack, dumped her art pens on the floor and began to plow through them.

Beezel didn't mind not going along with her parents, because two weeks in Baltimore was the perfect vacation for her. She loved cities. She wanted to visit all the great cities of the world. Rome. Paris. Beijing.

She looked over at Mimi. Beezel watched as Mimi took a strand of hair from the right side of her head. She twirled it around and around her forefinger.

Then she brought the end into her mouth and chewed on it.

There she goes again, Beezel thought. Chewing on your hair was disgusting. She had told Mimi that a million times.

Beezel sighed and decided to ignore her. She picked up a book titled *The Mystery of the Haunted Circus Tent*, settled into the sofa and began to read. She loved mysteries, and was just about to guess which clown was the bad guy when a strange scratching sound interrupted her.

Beezel looked around the small sitting room that connected the two bedrooms. One bedroom was for her and Mimi, and one was for Mr. Whaffle.

"Where *is* Mr. Whaffle?" she said. "I haven't seen him all afternoon."

"Oops," Mimi said. "I forgot to tell you." She opened the door to the sitting room closet and flipped on a light. A large wooden box, almost as tall as Beezel, sat on the floor. Muffled shouts came from inside.

"Mr. Whaffle is stuck," Mimi said. "While you were in the bathroom, I wanted to practice the Box of Doom. But Mr. Whaffle said he didn't want to. So

I ka-poofed him into a monkey."

The girls knew lots of magic tricks, but ka-poofing was *real* magic. "Ka-poofing" was the name the girls had given a magic gift that had been passed down to them when they were only seven.

"Not a monkey *again*," Beezel groaned.

"Actually, a chimpanzee." Mimi picked up one of the long silver swords that were stacked next to the box. "Then I put him in the box. I put a few swords through him here and there." She jabbed the box with the sword. "See?" She smiled proudly. "I'm getting pretty good at it."

Beezel put her hands on her hips. This was just like Mimi. She took a deep breath. She brushed her hair back with one hand. She counted to ten.

"Well," Mimi said. "You don't have to get mad about it. I *did* ka-poof him back." She shrugged. "But then I forgot how to open the box." Mimi sat back down on the floor, picked up her sketch pad and started doodling. She hummed. She looked up and gave Beezel a wide-eyed "What?" stare.

"Well, now you've done it," Beezel said. "You've ka-poofed him too many times this week. You know it's bad for his nerves." She cupped her hands and shouted at the box, "Don't worry, Mr. Whaffle! I'll get you out!"

Beezel cracked her knuckles. She shook her hands in front of her a few times and rubbed her palms together.

"Okay, here goes," she said. She handed her watch to Mimi. "Time me."

Mimi looked down at the watch. "One . . . two . . . three . . . go!"

Beezel's hands flew back and forth over the top as she worked the brass lock. The Box of Doom sprang open.

"Five seconds." Mimi handed Beezel the watch. "That's pretty fast."

"It just takes practice," Beezel said. She reached inside and took Mr. Whaffle's hand.

"You ungrateful girls," the large, round man sputtered as he squeezed out of the box. He stood up and stretched. He looked down at them. "After all I've done for you!"

Mr. Whaffle ran his fingers through his shoulder-length gray hair. He pulled a comb from his pocket and flicked it through his mustache and goatee.

Beezel watched as he checked himself in the

mirror. On the outside, Mr. Whaffle looked like Buffalo Bill. But on the inside, he reminded her of a fussy English butler.

Mr. Whaffle wore a brown buckskin jacket with fringe along the edge of each sleeve. He had on his favorite pair of pants: black jeans that the Wild Woman of Waco had embroidered with dozens of silver stars. And as always, he wore a long-sleeved shirt with pearl snaps up the front.

Beezel loved Mr. Whaffle's collection of bolo string ties. Today he wore a black braided tie topped with a jade turtle that nestled up against his collar.

The twins watched as their teacher wrestled a neatly folded red bandanna from his back pocket. "And all this animal hair!" He blew his nose with a loud honk. "Your parents will hear about this! You two have ka-poofed me for the last time!"

Mimi pulled a pocket watch out of her sleeve. It was Grandpa Trimoni's watch, gold with a bright emerald stone in the center of its case. A thick gold chain was attached to a loop at the top.

Mimi looked at Beezel and winked. Then she held the watch up in front of Mr. Whaffle. She swung it back and forth from its chain.

Beezel couldn't help but admire the way Mimi could hypnotize people. Grandpa Trimoni had been an incredible stage hypnotist, and he had wanted to teach his granddaughters what he knew. Mimi had hypnotized someone the first time she tried, but Beezel had never seemed to get the hang of it.

"You are getting sleepy," Mimi said to Mr. Whaffle.

"Sleepy," echoed Mr. Whaffle.

"So sleepy," Mimi said.

"So sleepy." Mr. Whaffle's eyes followed the watch.

"You are not mad at Beezel," Mimi said.

"Not mad at Beezel."

"You are not mad at Mimi."

"Not mad at Mimi."

"You would love to eat a pizza right now," Mimi said.

"Eat pizza now," Mr. Whaffle said drowsily.

"You will wake up when I count to three," said Mimi. "One . . . two . . . three!" She tucked the watch back inside her sleeve.

Mr. Whaffle pointed his finger at Mimi. "Furthermore!" He stopped. He rubbed his wide stomach with both hands. "What was I saying?"

"Furthermore," Beezel said.

"Oh, yes," Mr. Whaffle said. He blinked a couple of times. "Well . . ." He looked confused. "Well, don't you forget it!" He rubbed his stomach again. "I'm having a tremendous craving for a pizza. Would you girls like one?"

"Sure," said Mimi. "That's a great idea."

"With pepperoni," Beezel said. "And we'll come with you."

"Do you think we have time?" said Mr. Whaffle. "You can't be late for your opening night."

"There's plenty of time." Beezel reached for the door just as someone began to pound on it from the other side.

CHAPTER TWO

Beezel slowly opened their hotel room door. There, standing in the hall, was the strangest man she had ever seen.

To say he was tall would not be enough. To say he was thin would not be enough. To say he was mysterious and a little scary *still* would not be enough. He was all of these things, and something else.

The tall man bowed. A deep, sweeping bow. "Good evening," he said. "I am the Great Paparella."

His voice was smooth and soothing, like a lullaby. Beezel couldn't imagine a voice sounding more different from the way someone looked.

She studied his face. It was a thin face, just bone covered by skin. On his left cheek was an odd mark, shaped like two crescent moons sitting side by side.

The skin covering the mark was pink and shiny, almost iridescent.

She tried to figure out what could have made it. *Maybe he was in a sword fight.* No, it looked too intentional. *Is it a tattoo?* If it was, she couldn't quite make out what it was a tattoo of.

He saw her looking at his cheek, and his hand flew up to cover the strange mark. His eyes narrowed into slits.

"What are you staring at?" he said.

Beezel took a step back. "Nothing."

He snapped his eyes away from Beezel and focused them on Mr. Whaffle.

I've seen that mark somewhere before, she thought. *Now, where was it?*

Mr. Whaffle gently pushed her aside. "Please excuse their manners." He smiled and put out his hand. "These are the Trimoni Twins, Beezel and Mimi, and I am their teacher, Mr. Whaffle."

But the Great Paparella didn't take Mr. Whaffle's hand. He pulled away, as if Mr. Whaffle were some giant, round slug.

Instead he reached into his cape, whipped out a white envelope and handed it to him. Mr. Whaffle looked down at the envelope and back up again.

"As for them," the Great Paparella said, "I know who they are." He looked down at the twins. A slow smile spread across his face. "And soon," he said, "they will know *me*."

With that, he turned and seemed to vanish in a cloud of blue smoke.

"Well, he's not very friendly," Beezel said. "But he *is* fast." She poked her head out their hotel room door and peered down the long carpeted hallway. She saw the edge of his purple cape as he turned the corner.

"Oh, I just love blue smoke," sighed Mimi. "It's always such a nice effect. We should use blue smoke in our act, Beezel."

"What's inside the envelope?" asked Beezel.

Mr. Whaffle opened the envelope and pulled out a card. He cleared his throat and read:

"Merlin Hotels, Inc. is proud to announce that the Trimoni Twins have been challenged to a Magic Duel, to be held at our Baltimore hotel this Saturday at midnight.

The winner of this contest will be given a

year's membership to the exclusive Santini's Magic Club.

Only the judges and your teacher will be allowed to attend the competition.

If you do not attend, your opponent will win by default.

Your adversary will be the Great Paparella.

"You know," Mr. Whaffle said as he folded the card and handed it to Beezel, "being invited to a Magic Duel at the Merlin Hotel is quite an honor. The best magicians in the world have performed there."

Mr. Whaffle reached in his pocket and took out the small notebook he used to keep track of the twins' schedule. "Let's see," he said. "You're the first act here on Saturday night. That will give us plenty of time to get from the club to the Merlin Hotel by midnight." He looked down at the girls. "That is, if you want to do this. It's fine by me. And if you win . . . well, you can't buy publicity like that."

"Then let's do it, Beezel!" Mimi hopped up and down. "A Magic Duel. Onstage at *the* Merlin Hotel." She stopped jumping. "And I don't like that

Paparella one bit. Did you see how he treated Mr. Whaffle? Like he was a germ. Think of the fun we could have! We could ka-poof him into a camel! Or a hippo!"

"Well," Beezel said, "I didn't like him either. There's something about him . . ."

Saturday was just two days away. That wasn't very much time to get ready. But Mr. Whaffle was right: if they won, the publicity would be great for the Trimoni Circus.

Beezel wondered how Simon would have felt about a Magic Duel. After all, the only reason they knew how to ka-poof at all was because of Simon Serafin the Strong Man of the Trimoni Circus.

CHAPTER THREE

The twins had become friends with Simon the minute they met him. He told them stories about growing up stronger than anyone in the world.

"I could pick up both my parents when I was only three," he said. "I carried one under each arm, just like two loaves of bread."

The girls loved Simon and his stories. Simon loved the Trimoni Twins as if they were his own daughters.

Then one day Simon got very sick. Mr. and Mrs. Trimoni told the girls that he had asked to see them. Their parents watched as the girls walked across the field to Simon's trailer. Beezel knocked once and quietly opened the door.

"Sit next to me, girls," Simon said. While Beezel and Mimi sat on the edge of his bed, he told them about the Changing Coin.

"It's a fine thing to have," he said. "But to be honest, I've used it only once or twice." He tousled their hair. "I think two magicians such as yourselves could make better use of it. So I'm going to pass the gift on to you."

"But Simon," Mimi said, "what kind of gift is it? Is it a magic trick?"

"Is it hard to learn?" asked Beezel excitedly. She loved to learn new tricks. The harder the better.

"No," he said. "It's not a trick. It's *real* magic. Once you have the gift, you can change any living animal into another living animal. And then you can change it back." He rubbed his hand over his chin. "Let's see, how can I explain it?"

He looked at Mimi. "Let's say you want to turn Beezel into a lizard. First, you think the five magic words. Then you imagine a lizard. Then you point at Beezel. Ka-poof! Beezel will be a lizard."

"Could I turn Mimi into a gorilla?" asked Beezel.

"Of course," said Simon.

"Could I ka-poof Beezel into a giraffe?" asked Mimi.

"Absolutely," said Simon.

Beezel thought for a minute. "Can I turn myself into a warthog?"

"No," said Simon. "The magic doesn't work on you. Only on others."

Beezel scratched her head. "Can I ka-poof a cat into a person?"

"You can change a person into an animal, but not the other way around."

"Then can I turn *you* into Mr. Whaffle?" she asked.

"No." Simon chuckled. "Maybe the magician who made the Changing Coin didn't want anyone else that looked like him wandering around. You can't turn one human into another, but you *can* ka-poof a person into any other animal you please."

"But how do you ka-poof them back?" Mimi asked. "I wouldn't mind being a gorilla for a little while. But not forever."

"Just think the words in reverse order," said Simon. "And point. Then the animal will return to its original form."

He leaned over and took a small box from his nightstand. "This is what you use to pass on the gift." He opened the box.

He reached inside and took out an old bronze

coin. To Beezel it looked like something that should be in a museum.

There were words carved in a circle on one side. Just five words. In the center of the coin was stamped a design of a strange animal. The top of the animal looked like a cobra. The bottom looked like a lion.

"This coin was made when magic was still very much alive." He ran his finger over the words. "It has been given from one person to another for centuries."

Beezel looked at Mimi. Mimi looked at Beezel.

"So only one of us will get the gift?" Mimi asked. "Can I have it?"

Beezel rolled her eyes. She wondered what it would be like to be an only child. "Why should you have it?" she said. "I'd like it, too."

"Well, I'd be better at it," said Mimi. "I'm an artist. I'd think of better animals."

"You would not," said Beezel. Right now she was thinking of the perfect animal. A snail. An itty-bitty snail. A snail named Mimi.

"I would, too," said Mimi.

"Girls," he said. "Each of you will get the gift.

Because you are twins, part of your soul is shared. So you two count as one. Twins have always counted as one with the magic gift."

Simon held the coin up and smiled. "And the magic will be even more fun with the two of you." He turned his head to Mimi. "You will be able to change a duck into a horse . . ." He looked at Beezel. "And at the very same time *you* can turn a mouse into a buffalo."

"Wow," said Mimi.

He propped himself up on one elbow. "There are many things I cannot tell you about the magic. I know only what the person who gave *me* the gift told me. She was not a twin, but she did tell me this, and it is very important, so I want you to listen." He looked at the girls. "The magic works differently because you are twins."

"How?" Beezel asked.

"You must be together for the magic to work properly," he said. "When you are apart, the magic will grow weak."

"Will it work if I'm in the trailer and Mimi is outside?" asked Beezel.

"I'm not sure," said Simon. "I've never seen the

magic work with anyone else except for the person who gave the gift to me."

Beezel thought he looked sad. She reached over and touched his hand.

"Exactly how the magic works with twins," said Simon as he patted Beezel's hand, "is something that you and Mimi will have to find out for yourselves. There is no one alive who can give you all the answers."

Then he told them that they could never say the secret words out loud, or even write them down, because if they did, the magic of ka-poofing would die. The words could be spoken only to pass the gift on.

"You don't have to be near the coin to use its magic," Simon said. "But when the time comes for you to transfer the gift to someone else, both of you girls must touch the coin. The person receiving the gift must touch it as well. When you say the five words, the magic will leave you and enter that person."

Simon held the coin in the palm of his hand. He asked the girls to touch it. Beezel and Mimi each placed a finger on the coin.

"And as I say these words out loud," he said, "it will be for the first time . . . and for the last time. The magic will die for me, and the gift will belong to Beezel and Mimi Trimoni." He smiled at the girls. "Care for this gift, young Trimonis. Keep the coin well hidden. I ask only that when the time comes for you to pass it on, you give it to a good soul."

"We promise," said Beezel and Mimi.

And then he told them the five words.

"Hurry home," he said. "The gift is yours." He kissed them each on the cheek.

When the twins returned to their small bedroom at the back of their parents' trailer, they decided to try ka-poofing each other.

"I'll ka-poof you first," Mimi said. "What animal should I pick?"

"A cat," Beezel said. "A house cat so I'll fit in our room."

"How will I know when to ka-poof you back?" Mimi asked.

Beezel thought for a minute. "I'll lick your face."

"Okay. Here goes." Mimi ka-poofed Beezel into a cat.

In the split second it took for her to become a cat,

Beezel felt her whole body tingle. She felt warm and then slightly itchy all over as her skin and clothes instantly disappeared and were replaced by gray fur. It happened so quickly, and was such a surprise, that she found herself laughing out loud. But the sound she heard coming out of her mouth wasn't a laugh, it was a series of short mews.

Beezel stretched and admired her beautiful coat and long tail. She loved seeing the world from a cat's eyes as she jumped effortlessly from the bed to the dresser and back again. She liked it so much she purred.

It was wonderful to be herself, and yet be a cat. But there was still a difference, however small. A tiny part of her mind was thinking about hunting and eating the mouse that she had seen scurry across the circus tent floor that morning.

Before she licked Mimi's face to signal her to ka-poof her back, Beezel wanted to test something. She wanted to see if she could ka-poof Mimi as well. She thought the words, imagined a cat and pointed her paw at Mimi from across the room. Nothing. She sat on Mimi's lap, thought the words, imagined a cat and pointed her paw at her. Still nothing.

She licked Mimi's face. Mimi ka-poofed her back. She was Beezel again.

"Wow!" said Beezel. "That was more fun than conjuring catfish!"

"Get off me!" Mimi said as she shoved Beezel off her lap.

"Sorry," Beezel said. Then she told Mimi about testing the magic. "I don't think you can ka-poof while you're changed. So we should never ka-poof each other at the same time, because I think we would stay that way forever."

"Deal," Mimi said as she stood in the middle of the room. "Now it's my turn. Change me into a dog. I can't wait!"

Beezel ka-poofed Mimi into a small white dog. But instead of wagging her tail, Mimi ran in circles and yipped. She scratched herself madly with her hind legs.

Then Mimi tilted her head back and howled. It was a miserable cry, and when Beezel heard it, she quickly changed Mimi back.

"What happened?" Beezel asked her.

"It was awful," Mimi said. "While I was changing, I started to tingle and then itch all over."

"Me, too," Beezel said.

"But it got worse and worse. I itched everywhere. My nose, the tip of my tail. I couldn't scratch all the places that itched."

Beezel shook her head. "That didn't happen with me. Maybe I did something wrong. Let's try again."

This time Beezel changed Mimi into an iguana. *Maybe the fur was the problem,* she thought. But Mimi's eyes widened, and she ran in circles, so Beezel changed her back.

"It happened again," Mimi said as she scratched the back of her neck. "It's just not fair. *I'm* the one who loves animals. *I* should get to be one. But it just feels horrible."

"Maybe you're allergic to ka-poofing," Beezel said thoughtfully. She patted Mimi on the shoulder. "I know just how you feel. I feel like that when I eat pineapple. The roof of my mouth itches like crazy."

"Allergic," Mimi said sadly. "I can't believe it."

"Do you want to try one more time?" Beezel asked.

"No!" Mimi said. "Promise me you won't ka-poof me unless you absolutely have to. I can't stand the way it feels. It's like my skin is burning."

"I promise," Beezel said.

Later that night, Mr. and Mrs. Trimoni came into their room to tell them that Simon had died. It was the saddest day of Beezel and Mimi's lives. After the funeral, the twins told their parents about the Changing Coin.

Mr. Trimoni said, "We're going to keep this gift a secret, girls. Only our circus family will know about it. We mustn't tell outsiders. It's a powerful thing Simon has left you. We must protect it."

He put his arms around them. "And always keep your promise to Simon."

Ever since that day, the girls had worked hard to improve their ka-poofing skills. But now, looking down at the card from the Great Paparella, Beezel felt funny. She had never been nervous about ka-poofing before. They had ka-poofed onstage hundreds of times. But something was different about this.

"Come on, Beezel," Mimi said. "It'll be fun!"

"I'm not sure, Mimi," she said. "I'm not sure this is a good idea at all."

CHAPTER FOUR

Beezel and Mimi sat at their dressing table. It was almost showtime, the opening night for the Trimoni Twins at the Sleight of Hand Magic Club.

Mimi ran a comb through her hair. She slipped on a long, flowing silk jacket. She pulled on a pair of fire-engine-red boots. She hummed and sketched Beezel.

Beezel added a rose clip to the end of her braid. She put on her black bow tie and her matching satin jacket. She pulled on her shiny black boots. She made a list of the tricks they were to do that night and went over them carefully one by one.

"Are you sure you're ready?" said Beezel. She couldn't understand why Mimi never worried about a show. *Well,* she thought, *maybe I worry enough for both of us.*

"Ready," Mimi said happily.

"Where's Mr. Whaffle?" Beezel asked.

"He went to get Ricky and Lucy," Mimi said.

Ricky and Lucy were the girls' pygmy goats. The hotel manager had decided the girls had enough animals in their room, so Mr. Whaffle had set up a small pen for them in the prop room down the hall from the stage.

"Let's go see who's performing," Mimi said.

"We're not supposed to," Beezel said. "We might get in the way."

"But it's our opening night," said Mimi. "Don't you want to see the first act? Don't you think we should check out our competition? Please! I can't stand sitting here any longer."

Beezel looked at her watch. They had fifteen minutes before their act started.

"I guess it can't hurt," she said. "But you have to be very quiet, or the stagehands will tell Mr. Whaffle on us. Promise?" She stuck out her pinkie finger.

"Promise," said Mimi. She grabbed Beezel's little finger with hers and shook it. "Pinkie swear on Merlin's underwear."

Tiptoeing in boots is never easy, but the twins tried their best. They crept to the back of the stage. A red velvet curtain hung down to the floor in front of them. They could hear someone talking. But they couldn't see a thing.

"Who is it?" whispered Mimi.

"Shh," said Beezel. She pointed down.

Beezel lay down on her stomach. She pulled up the tiniest bit of the curtain—just enough so she could see the stage. A magician had his back to them. Beezel could see that he was tall and thin. He had black hair and a long purple cape.

He was pointing a wand at a floating teacup. When he pointed to the left, the cup floated to the left. When he pointed to the right, the cup floated to the right.

She motioned for Mimi to look. Mimi lay close to Beezel. The two girls peeked out together.

"There's a good crowd," whispered Beezel. "There are about twenty people in one row, and let's see, there's ten, fifteen rows . . ."

"Don't count them!" hissed Mimi. "You know it's bad luck to count the audience."

"Sorry," whispered Beezel. "I just can't help it sometimes."

The magician pointed to a tall black hat that sat on the table. The teacup floated down inside it.

"Not bad," whispered Beezel.

"Salami, salami, baloney," whispered Mimi. "Anybody can do *that*."

The magician bowed and turned to walk off the stage. The twins saw his face.

"Paparella!" Beezel and Mimi said at the same time.

Beezel looked at her watch. "Great Rami Sami's turban! Come on, we're late!" She grabbed Mimi's arm. They ran to the stage entrance. Mr. Whaffle was there, nervously tapping his foot.

"There you are," he scolded. "I had to get the animals set up by myself." He sneezed and blew his nose. "That is *not* very professional of you."

"Sorry," Mimi said. She reached in her sleeve for her pocket watch.

"Geez, not now, Mimi!" said Beezel. "It's time to go on!"

Beezel shoved Mimi up the stairs and onto the stage.

The footlights went up. Beezel looked out at the crowd. She was right—the club was packed. Not one empty seat, not even in the very back. Beezel bet there were at least three hundred seats in the small theater, but there was no time for counting. She'd ask Mr. Whaffle later.

The audience began to clap. Beezel and Mimi smiled at each other. It was always like this. Every time they did magic, they felt magical, too.

The twins loved magic so much that they would have gladly performed all night, but Mr. Whaffle was very strict. Thirty minutes and that was it. So Mimi and Beezel spent their time trying to do as many tricks as possible.

Mimi pulled twenty-four doves out of a hat. Then Beezel made them disappear again, one by one. Beezel put Mimi in the Box of Doom. Mimi did mind-reading tricks. They did all their favorites. And they saved ka-poofing for last.

Mimi came onstage with Ricky and Lucy. "And now," she said, "before your very eyes, we will make these little goats fly!"

Beezel glanced at Mimi. They had never done this particular ka-poofing trick in front of an audience before. Of course they had practiced it many times, to get the goats used to being ka-poofed. But Beezel was still a little nervous. Then Mimi smiled at her and she felt better. Her confidence was contagious.

Beezel knelt beside Ricky. "It's okay, boy," she said, scratching his ear. "Just come when I call you."

Mimi and Beezel looked at each other. Mimi held up her hand. She put one finger up, then two, then three. Three fingers was the signal for them to each think the five secret words, imagine a bird and then point at their goat.

Ka-poof. Beezel changed Ricky into a blue parakeet. Ka-poof. Mimi changed Lucy into a yellow canary. The two birds flew up to the ceiling and perched on a chandelier.

Beezel held up her hand. She put one finger up, then two, then three. Three fingers was the signal to change them into butterflies. They pointed at the birds.

Ka-poof. Beezel changed Ricky into a bright orange butterfly. Ka-poof. Mimi changed Lucy into a yellow-and-black-striped butterfly.

"Come on back, girl!" Mimi said to Lucy.

"Come here, Ricky!" Beezel said as she waved two carrots in the air. "That's a boy!"

The butterflies slowly fluttered back to the stage floor.

"And now, we'd like our goats back," said Mimi.

She held up her fingers. One, two, three. They pointed at the butterflies.

Ka-poof. Ricky and Lucy were goats again.

The audience exploded in applause.

"You're glad to be back, aren't you boy?" Beezel said as she patted Ricky's back. She gave each of the goats a carrot.

"Bravo! Encore!" the audience shouted as Beezel and Mimi took a bow. Someone tossed a bouquet of roses for each twin onto the stage.

The twins smiled, picked up the roses and waved back at the cheering crowd. It had been a great show. Nothing was better than performing magic onstage.

Mimi and Beezel held hands and bowed again. Then they turned and led their goats offstage. Mr. Whaffle was waiting for them.

"You did a good job tonight, girls," he said. "Now someone wants to see you, Mimi."

"Gumdrop!" said Mimi.

"I think she's feeling better," Mr. Whaffle said as he wrapped the big snake around her shoulders.

"That was impressive," a voice behind him said. "Very impressive. I especially liked that last trick." Paparella stepped between the twins and Mr. Whaffle. He stared down at their hands. "It's as if you had the power to actually transform those beasts."

Paparella looked at Gumdrop and wrinkled his nose. "Snakes. I detest those creatures." He leaned over and inspected the snake's skin. "Well, it *would* make a lovely pair of boots." He laughed.

Mimi's face turned bright red. She glared at Paparella. "This is *my* snake," she said. "And if you hurt her, I'll . . . I'll . . ."

"She's a much beloved pet, Mr. Paparella," interrupted Mr. Whaffle. "And now if you'll excuse us, it's time these girls went to bed."

Mr. Whaffle walked the twins down the hall to their dressing room. "I'll take the goats back to their pen," he said. "You girls change your clothes and meet me back up in the room."

"Just let him try to make boots out of Gumdrop,"

Mimi muttered as she stomped into their dressing room.

Beezel started to follow her in, then stopped. She looked back down the hall to the stage. The Great Paparella was still there. And she didn't like the way he was smiling.

CHAPTER FIVE

The next morning, Beezel decided to find out more about Paparella. There was just something about him she didn't like. The first person she wanted to talk to was Hector.

Hector knew about every magician in the country. In his spare time, when he wasn't running the midway for the Trimoni Circus, Hector wrote biographies about magicians. If anyone would know about the Great Paparella, he would.

She called Hector's trailer at the circus camp in Baraboo. There was no answer. Beezel left a message asking him to call her back. She walked back into their bedroom. Mimi sat curled up on the bed wrapped in a blanket. Just her nose and eyes peeked out.

"I wish I could talk to Dad," Beezel said. "I bet he knows about Paparella."

"Tell Mr. Whaffle you want to call them," Mimi said. "He has their number."

"I don't want to bother them. Not when they're out scouting for talent," said Beezel.

"Well, I don't know why *we* can't know where they are," Mimi said. "It's not like we'd tell anyone."

"I know." Beezel kicked off her slippers and crawled back into bed. "Maybe they'll call us after Dad is done tackling a yeti."

"And Mom is finished arm wrestling the poor thing to get it to sign up with our circus," said Mimi.

Mimi looked at Beezel. Beezel looked at Mimi. The two girls burst into laughter.

The bedroom door opened. Mr. Whaffle was holding a tray. On it was a pot of hot chocolate, a plate of toast and a newspaper.

"Well, you two are certainly in good spirits," he said. "Considering."

"Considering what?" asked Beezel.

"Considering this." He handed her the morning

paper from the tray. He had circled a section in red. "Read the review of last night's performance."

Mimi read out loud:

"Last night at the Sleight of Hand Magic Club, the audience was witness to a halfhearted attempt at magic by the Trimoni Twins. After a faulty start, the two young magicians managed to pull off a few mediocre tricks. But all in all, it was a fairly boring performance."

"Sim sala bim!" said Beezel. "What does it mean, 'a faulty start'?"

"Yeah," said Mimi. "We were good. And what does some newspaper guy know about magic, anyway?"

"You're right," Beezel said. "It's not like *he's* a magician."

"Girls," Mr. Whaffle interrupted. He placed the tray on the nightstand. "I think you're missing something." He pointed to the headline of the article. It said,

"MAGIC ON THE TOWN" BY THE GREAT PAPARELLA

Underneath was a small photograph of the magician.

"It's him!" said Mimi.

"But it's all lies," Beezel said. "The show was great. Everyone loved us!"

"Evidently, not *everyone*," said Mr. Whaffle.

"He makes me so mad," Mimi said. She stood up on the bed and shook one fist in the air. "By the powers of Siegfried and Roy . . . we are not boring!"

"You are many things, young Trimoni Twins," said Mr. Whaffle as he poured them each a cup of hot chocolate. "Boring is *not* one of them."

"Thanks, Mr. Whaffle," said Mimi.

Beezel climbed out of bed. She put her hands on her hips and looked at Mimi.

"You know, I think Mom and Dad would want us to compete," she said. "Let's give the Great Paparella his Magic Duel!"

"Yes!" Mimi stood and bounced up and down on the bed.

"Well, now that that's been decided, let's eat," said Mr. Whaffle. He moved a white dove off the corner of the nightstand and served the girls their buttered toast.

* * *

After breakfast, they had to do their schoolwork in the hotel room. Mr. Whaffle tried his best to fill their heads with fractions and decimals, but Beezel couldn't stop thinking about the Great Paparella. Why had he lied about their show?

And Hector. Could he tell her about Paparella? It might help to know what kind of magic tricks he usually did. Then she and Mimi could make a plan for the Magic Duel.

Beezel looked over at Mimi. Her art pens were scattered on the floor in front of her. She was drawing a picture of Gumdrop. And she was tapping her foot. *And* she was chewing on a piece of her hair.

At least I know how to pretend *I'm listening,* thought Beezel.

Mr. Whaffle glanced down at his watch. "It's almost noon," he said. "I know when I'm beaten." He took out a bandanna and patted his forehead. "We are not getting anywhere in the world of math today." He leaned over and examined Mimi's drawing. "Although we've made some strides in the realm of art."

Mr. Whaffle didn't seem to have his heart in

teaching. Once he'd been the premier knife thrower in the world.

Mr. Trimoni had told the girls, "When Mr. Whaffle performed, he was powerful and quick, like a cat. You wouldn't have recognized him."

But then one day, he pierced the Amazing Aqua Boy's flipper. It was just a small nick, and the Aqua Boy was fine. He swam in his tank that very same day. But after that, Mr. Whaffle lost his nerve.

"Which is a very bad thing for a knife thrower to lose," Mrs. Trimoni had said.

Luckily, Mr. Whaffle was also a very smart man. Mr. Trimoni put him in charge of the Trimoni Circus finances and made him the teacher of the children in the circus.

Beezel looked at him now. He ran his fingers through his long hair. He straightened his mustache.

"I think you two need some fresh air," he said. "Why don't you get yourselves some lunch? Then take a brisk walk and meet me back here at two."

"That's a great idea," Mimi said. "Can we bring you back something?"

"No," he said. "I think I need some fresh air

of my own." He put on his hat and walked out of the room.

Mimi picked up something from her lap. It was round and furry.

"What's that?" Beezel pointed to the hairy ball.

"It's a chinchilla," Mimi said. "And it's time to ka-poof her back."

"Mimi, what have you done *now*?" asked Beezel.

"While you were in the shower, the maid came in. She wanted to make the bed." Mimi shrugged. "But I was still sleepy."

"Mimi," said Beezel. "You don't ka-poof someone just for the heck of it. Un-ka-poof her right now."

"I was going to anyway, Miss Bossy." Mimi pointed at the little animal.

Ka-poof. A very confused hotel maid looked down at them. She squealed once and scratched behind one ear. Beezel knew exactly what she was going through. It took a few seconds after getting ka-poofed to know whether you were a human again, or still a chinchilla.

Mimi smiled sweetly at the maid. "Do you need to make the bed?"

"Did you just . . . ?" said the maid.

"You'd better get your watch," sighed Beezel.

Mimi pulled her pocket watch out of her sleeve. She waved the watch back and forth.

"You are getting sleepy," said Mimi.

"Sleepy," said the maid.

"You were never a chinchilla," said Mimi.

"Never a chinchilla," said the maid.

"You will leave Mimi two chocolates on her pillow tonight," said Mimi.

"Two chocolates for Mimi," said the maid.

While she waited for Mimi to send the maid on her way, Beezel admired the tall buildings from the view out their hotel window.

"Hurry up, Mimi," Beezel said. "I want to go outside and look around. Just look at all those people! And there's a park up the street we can walk to."

"Let me tuck Gumdrop in first," Mimi said as she put her snake inside the carrier and pushed it toward the entry closet.

The girls took the props they would need for the show that night out of the closet before putting the carrier in. Beezel waited patiently in the sitting room while Mimi talked softly to Gumdrop. But then she heard Mimi begin to sing the snake a lullaby.

"Willard the Wizard's wristwatch!" yelled Beezel. "Hurry up already!"

"Shh!" Mimi said as she came out of the closet. "Have a nice nap!" she whispered to Gumdrop as she closed the closet door behind her.

CHAPTER SIX

The girls raced down the hotel stairs instead of taking the elevator. Mr. Whaffle insisted on it. He wanted them to stay in top form for their act.

Mimi opened the door to the street. A cool autumn breeze washed over them.

"What a beautiful day!" she said. She grabbed Beezel's arm and whirled her around.

"And we don't have to be back until two!" Beezel said. It felt great to be out of the hotel room. She just wished they had time to go to a museum, too. There was one up the street from their hotel. She hoped Mr. Whaffle would take them there soon.

"Mr. Whaffle!" She slapped her forehead. "Oops, I forgot to ask him for lunch money."

Mimi looked in her pockets. She pulled a pack of

chewing gum out of one. She found a small brown mouse in the other.

"Oh, there you are, Caesar," she said. She tucked him back inside.

"Mimi," Beezel said, feeling slightly panicked at the sight of Mimi's empty pockets. "Where is the Changing Coin? I gave it to you this morning. Please, please, please don't tell me you've lost it!"

Mr. Trimoni had taught them to hide the coin in their trailer at home, but for the next two weeks, he wanted the girls to keep the coin with them. "Just ka-poof anyone that gets too close," he said. "And ask questions later. It's the best protection you can give Simon's coin."

"No, I didn't lose it, Miss Worrywart," Mimi said. "I hid it back in the room before we left. I want to swing on the bars at the park, and I thought it would fall out when I hung upside down."

Beezel sighed with relief. "But what about poor Caesar? Did you think about him? That's going to give him a pretty big headache."

"Oh." Mimi giggled. "Yeah. I guess I'll skip the bars."

Beezel reached down into one pocket and pulled

out a few dollars. She reached down into the other and pulled out two quarters and a nickel.

"Too bad ka-poofing doesn't work with money," Mimi said. "If it did, we could go eat some seafood. And I heard there's a cruise that goes around the harbor." She stuck out her lower lip.

"Oh, for Aladdin's kneecaps!" said Beezel. She jammed her money down into her sweater pocket. "Who needs a harbor cruise? Let's go for a walk. And we can stop at the restaurant next to the hotel and get some soup to take back to our room. We have enough for that."

They linked arms and walked side by side. Mimi hummed and kicked the leaves as she walked. Beezel watched the leaves swirling to the ground. She was careful not to step on them, or any of the cracks in the sidewalk either.

Soon Beezel had a feeling that someone was following them. She stopped and turned around.

"What's wrong?" asked Mimi.

People filed past them. Tall, short, old, young. No one looked familiar.

"I don't know," Beezel said. "I thought we were being followed."

"But that's just silly," Mimi said. "Who would follow us? You've been reading too many mysteries." She ran ahead of Beezel. "Race you!"

Beezel stood for a moment longer, looking at the busy street. Then she shrugged, turned and started to chase Mimi to the park. But as she did, she felt someone tug hard at her sweater and reach down inside her pocket.

Beezel turned and yanked her sweater away. She scanned the busy sidewalk. People jostled against her. Whoever it was had gone. But she thought she saw the edge of a familiar purple cape as it disappeared into the crowd.

She turned and ran to her sister. "Mimi! Stop!" She grabbed Mimi's arm. "Someone robbed me!"

"*Robbed* you? Are you sure?" said Mimi. "What did they take?"

Beezel reached inside her pockets. The dollar bills were still there, but the two quarters and the nickel were gone.

"Well, I'll be Hackaliah Bailey's elephant!" Beezel said. "He just took the coins."

"I guess he isn't the smartest thief in the city," Mimi said, laughing.

"I guess so," Beezel said. "Do you think we should tell the police?"

"For fifty-five cents?" said Mimi. "Not me. I'm going to the park." She ran ahead.

Beezel stood and watched her for a minute.

It wasn't much money, but still, it had scared her. And there was that bit of purple she had caught a glimpse of. She couldn't be sure it was a cape, of course. There were lots of purple jackets and coats in a big city. She shook her head.

Mimi's probably right, she told herself. *He just wasn't a very good thief.* She ran after Mimi to the park. But she couldn't shake the feeling that some-one might be running after *her.*

CHAPTER SEVEN

Later, when they got back to their hotel room, Beezel checked at the front desk for a message from Hector. There was nothing.

"And nothing from Mom and Dad either," she said to Mimi.

They sat cross-legged on the floor and ate their cups of crab soup. Beezel had bought a loaf of bread to go with it. She broke off a piece and handed it to Mimi.

"Why do you think someone picked my pocket?" Beezel asked. "I mean, I'm eleven years old. How much money could I possibly have?"

"I don't know why you keep talking about it," Mimi said. She took the bread and dunked it into her cup. "This *is* the city, after all. Cities have pickpockets. Why does everything have to mean something?"

"Because," said Beezel. She blew across the top of her soup to cool it. "It usually does."

"Can we please talk about something else?" Mimi slurped down the last of her soup and wiped her mouth on her sleeve. "Let's talk about the Magic Duel. What trick should we do first?"

"Hmm?" Beezel tried to concentrate. She was still thinking about the pickpocket. "Oh, I don't know. We need something really exciting. Something that will impress the judges." She stood up, picked up their trash and threw it in the wastebasket. "I wish we had one of our elephants. We could make it disappear."

"I have an idea," said Mimi. "Let's cut someone in half!" She thought for a minute. "How about Mr. Whaffle?"

Beezel giggled. "Do you think he'd let you?"

"Sure," Mimi said. "He's one hundred percent circus inside. He loves a good show as much as we do." She stood up and twirled around. "Presenting the Two Halves of Mr. Whaffle!" she yelled. She waved her hand to the left. "First, for your amazement, is

Mr. Whaffle's top half!" She waved her hand to the right. "And now, ladies and gentlemen, even more incredible, Mr. Whaffle's bottom half!"

Beezel whistled and clapped. Mimi bowed.

"Well, if you're sure you want to do it," said Beezel, "then *you* ask him."

"Okay, I will," said Mimi. "But then *I* get to cut him in half, not you."

"Be my guest." Beezel laughed and looked at her watch. It was almost two forty-five. "Where *is* Mr. Whaffle? He's never this late. I'm getting worried about him."

Mimi looked at Beezel. "Me, too," she said.

Some people chew their fingernails when they're nervous. And some people pace back and forth. But the Trimoni Twins practiced magic.

Mimi practiced ka-poofing. She took Gadget out of her cage. Ka-poof. Gadget was a penguin. Then she ka-poofed her back. Ka-poof. Llama. Ka-poof. Back. Ka-poof. Anteater. Ka-poof. Back.

Beezel practiced juggling. She juggled their schoolbooks. She juggled a chair, the wastebasket and Mimi's makeup case.

"Don't drop my case," Mimi said.

"I never drop anything," Beezel said as she threw it in the air. "I am the Great Beezel Trimoni!"

Just then, the door to their room flew open. Beezel dropped the makeup case, the chair and the wastebasket. Before them stood Mr. Whaffle. A very scared, out-of-breath Mr. Whaffle.

"Are you girls all right?" gasped Mr. Whaffle. "I've been worried sick." He hugged them both and then collapsed in a round heap on the sitting room sofa.

"We're fine," Beezel said. "But where have *you* been?"

"I took a short walk and came back to the hotel. Someone called here and said there had been an accident at the park. That you were hurt. I ran all the way there. But the park police said there hadn't been an accident at all. They said it must have been a prank phone call. I wasn't sure, so I ran all the way back here."

Beezel couldn't imagine Mr. Whaffle running anywhere. He was nearly as wide as he was tall. Just the walk down the stairs got him huffing and puffing.

"Who do you think called?" asked Beezel. She told him about the walk to the park. How she felt like they were being followed. And about her missing fifty-five cents.

"Well," said Mr. Whaffle, "maybe it's nothing at all. Just a string of coincidences. But let's be careful, just in case. I don't want you two to go anywhere without me."

Mimi groaned. But Beezel agreed. They wouldn't go anywhere alone.

Mr. Whaffle sat up and coughed. Beezel could tell he was still out of breath. "Shall we get back to our studies?" he wheezed as he flipped open a thick book on the coffee table. "We still haven't reviewed for the science test I'm going to give you next week."

Mimi groaned even louder. "Do we *have* to? Can't we go *do* something?"

"I have an idea," said Beezel. "Why don't we go on a field trip?"

"Well, that could be educational," said Mr. Whaffle. "What did you have in mind? The Maryland Science Center?"

"Oh no," said Mimi. "Not another science museum! I'd rather go to the laundromat and wash our clothes." She stuck out her lower lip.

"There is a museum I'd like to see," Beezel said to Mr. Whaffle. "And it's only a few miles from here."

Mr. Whaffle looked suspicious. "And the name of it would be?"

"The Museum of the Strange and Magical." Beezel tried to make it sound as educational as possible.

Mr. Whaffle looked at his fingernails. "The Strange and Magical. And exactly how does that fit into your curriculum?"

Beezel scratched behind one ear. "Well . . ."

"Career advancement!" Mimi said, perking up. "We can use the field trip to further our careers as magicians!"

"Yes!" said Beezel. Sometimes Mimi surprised her. "*And* it's the study of history as well. Think of all the fantastic magicians who came before us." She waved her hand. "Carter the Great."

Mimi twirled. "Harry Blackstone."

Beezel bowed. "And David Copperfield."

Mr. Whaffle smiled. "I guess it won't hurt to spend a couple of hours there."

"Yes!" Mimi threw her fist in the air.

"Thank you!" Beezel said.

On the cab ride over to the museum, Beezel chatted with Mimi. "I've read about this museum. It sounds great," she said. "They even have some of Houdini's things." Mimi was a big Houdini fan.

"Houdini!" said Mimi. "Oh my gosh! Just think, we're going to get to see something that Harry Houdini actually *touched*!"

The museum was tucked between a Chinese take-out restaurant on one side and a coffeehouse on the other. It was a tall brick building, several stories high, with a flat roof. In the center of the building was a small covered porch flanked by two tall columns.

Beezel lifted the brass knocker on the door and rapped it against the wood. The door opened immediately. A man in a black suit and red bow tie greeted them.

"Welcome to my museum," he said. "I am Professor Finkleroy." He waved them in. "Please come in and look around."

While Mr. Whaffle paid for their tickets, Beezel and Mimi stepped inside the dimly lighted building. On their left was a small lobby and reception area. To their right was a gift shop. Straight ahead was a set of double doors. The girls pushed them open and went into the main hall. On each side of the hallway were display rooms.

The first room they entered had a sign above the door that said CABINETS OF WONDER. It was lined with shelves that held the remains of strange creatures. Beezel read the label on one: "Three-headed tree frog, found Topanga, California, 1931."

"Yuck," whispered Mimi.

"Triple yuck," Beezel whispered back.

"All right, girls," Mr. Whaffle said as he came up behind them. "I have a map of the museum. Where should we go first?"

The twins agreed to see the displays about magic on the second floor first and then work their way up. If there was any time left, they would see the life-size Alien Encounters diorama on the fourth floor.

They climbed the stairs to the second floor. As they opened the stairwell door and stepped out into the hall, Beezel saw Professor Finkleroy, the same man who had just sold them tickets.

"Would you like to see our Harry Houdini collection?" he said. "We've got a few pieces on loan from some private parties and museums."

"Yes, please!" Mimi said.

"I'm sure it's very educational," Beezel added

quickly for Mr. Whaffle's benefit.

Professor Finkleroy led them down the hall and into a small room. Along the walls were Houdini's Metamorphosis Trunk, the Chinese Water Torture Cell and several glass display cases. Inside the cases were Houdini's collections of locks and keys, hand-cuffs, leg irons, and one of his straitjackets.

When they came out of the exhibit, Professor Finkleroy turned to Mimi. "I hope you enjoyed it," he said.

"Are you kidding?" Mimi said. "I love Houdini. He's my very favorite magician of all time."

"Well, there are a few more of Houdini's things in the case over there." He pointed across the hall. "And don't forget to look at the photos of famous magicians' pets. They're right next door."

"Thanks!" Mimi said as she ran over to the case. Mr. Whaffle followed her.

"And as for you," Professor Finkleroy said to Beezel, "I think you'd be interested in some old magicians' posters I have. They're hanging up along this hallway."

"Thanks," Beezel said. She didn't want to hurt his feelings, but posters were the last thing in the museum she wanted to see. She quickly glanced at each poster as she walked down the hall with Professor Finkleroy, pretending to be interested. But then something caught her eye and she stopped to look. The poster in front of her read:

THE GREAT PAPARELLA

IN HIS FINAL APPEARANCE

APRIL 10TH THROUGH 20TH, 1902

"The Great Paparella!" Beezel stared at the picture on the poster. A fat, jolly-looking magician with flaming red hair smiled back at her. "But that's not him." She examined the happy Paparella in the old poster. "But if this is the *real* Great Paparella, then who is the other one?"

She turned to Professor Finkleroy for an answer, but he had disappeared.

CHAPTER EIGHT

That night they ate Chinese take-out food in their hotel room. While she ate, Beezel wondered why the Great Paparella was using another magician's name. Unless the real Great Paparella was his relative—but they sure didn't look alike.

Mimi picked at her sesame chicken and ate her white rice. "I miss macaroni and cheese. The way Emmett makes it in the cook tent."

Beezel laughed. "It's a good thing we're identical twins," she said. She popped a spicy shrimp into her mouth. "Otherwise people would never know we're related."

"I just like my food plain," said Mimi. She picked the sliced green onions off her chicken and put them on a paper napkin. "Is that some kind of crime?"

"Girls," said Mr. Whaffle. "Eat. You have to get ready for your show soon."

The phone rang and the desk clerk said a gentleman was waiting for them in the lobby.

"Who do you think it is?" said Mimi. "Mr. Paparella?"

"I don't know," said Mr. Whaffle. "But let's go meet him together."

The twins put their take-out boxes on the coffee table.

Mr. Whaffle led the way to the elevator. "I think we've had our exercise for the day."

In the center of the lobby was a green armchair. Sitting in it was a small man with wild white hair. He had very unusual eyes. They were pink.

"Hector!" Mimi ran to him and scooped him up.

"Put me down!" said Hector. "That is a very undignified thing for you to do!"

"Hector!" Beezel leaned over and gave him a hug. "We've missed you so much! How are Mom and Dad? Have you heard from them?"

Hector's lip quivered. "I have bad news."

Beezel gasped. "Has something happened to them?"

"No, no, duckie. I didn't mean to worry you," Hector said with a sigh. He wiped his eyes.

"Please don't cry, Hector," said Mimi. "It can't be that bad."

"Oh, but it is," Hector said. "Someone has broken into your parents' trailer at the circus. I hadn't checked inside the trailer for a few days, so last night I did. Someone had destroyed everything. They cut up the bedding and broke all your mother's nice things." He looked at Beezel. "But not one thing was stolen. The person who broke in was looking for something."

"Our coin?" asked Beezel.

"I think so. I got here as soon as I could." He looked at the girls with fierce determination. "And now that I'm here, I'll protect you."

"But it's impossible that anyone else would find out," said Mr. Whaffle. "The only people who know about the coin are you, me, the girls and their parents. And we haven't told anyone."

"I didn't tell a soul," said Hector.

"Do you know who did it?" Beezel asked him.

Hector shook his head. "After I found the mess in your parents' trailer," he said, "I asked around the camp to see if anyone had seen anything. That's when Hillary said she had seen a man outside one of the trailers a few days before. She said he was being nosy so she told him to get off the property right then and there. Hillary doesn't like strangers. And I guess he didn't argue."

"No one argues with Hillary," Mimi said. Hillary was the circus's bearded lady.

Hector nodded. "She's as strong as an ox, that girl," he said. "So I asked her what this stranger looked like. She said he was tall and thin and had a funny mark on his left cheek."

Beezel turned to Mimi.

"Paparella," they said at the same time.

"Or whoever he *really* is," added Beezel. "That's who I was calling you about, Hector." She showed him the picture of Paparella from the newspaper.

"That might be him," Hector said. "It sure looks like the man Hillary described."

"Do you know the Great Paparella?" asked Beezel. "He's a magician. Have you ever written about him?"

"I've never seen him before." Hector scratched his head. "I think there was a Paparella once, but it was a while back."

Beezel nodded. "This Paparella looks completely different from that Paparella."

Hector looked at Mr. Whaffle. "I'll have to call Eric and Frederica and tell them."

"Of course, of course." Mr. Whaffle flipped open his notebook and jotted down a number. He ripped out the page and handed it to Hector. "If you don't feel up to calling them, I will."

"No." Hector shook his head. "It's my job to call them."

Mr. Whaffle insisted he come up to their room and spend the night.

"Why don't you rest for a little while," Beezel told Hector when they got back to the room, "and we'll talk more after the show."

Mr. Whaffle closed the door to his bedroom and joined the girls in the sitting room.

"Girls," he said, "I don't like this one bit. I think you're in great danger."

CHAPTER NINE

The twins got a standing ovation after their act that night, but Beezel found it very hard to concentrate on magic. She kept wondering if Paparella was in the wings watching them.

Mr. Whaffle was so worried that he held the girls' hands on the way back to their rooms, something Beezel couldn't remember him doing since they were five.

When they got inside, Hector was awake and waiting for them. "Did the show go all right?" he asked. "I called your parents. They weren't in, but I left a message."

"The show was fine," Beezel said.

Mr. Whaffle paced across the sitting room. The fringe on his jacket swayed back and forth with him.

While he walked, he mumbled under his breath. Beezel couldn't hear what he was saying, but it didn't matter. Her mind was on other things.

Mimi sat cross-legged on the sofa. "Everything of Mom's was destroyed," she said sadly. "That means the porcelain frogs she's collected since she was a little girl. And the tiny tea set that Uncle Remkin brought her from China. The beautiful silk saris that Siyan the Snake Charmer gave her for her birthday. Ruined." She put her head in her hands. "Poor Mom."

Beezel walked over and sat next to Mimi. She put her arm around her. She was thinking about Paparella. What an awful thing to do. But what he wanted wasn't in her parents' trailer. She felt sure of that. But that meant . . .

Beezel jumped up. "The coin!" She turned to Mimi. "Where did you hide it?"

Mimi twirled her hair. "I . . . uh . . ."

Beezel threw her hands up in the air. "Mimi! Are you going to tell us *where*?"

"Geez, Beezel, you know I can't think when I'm nervous."

Beezel counted to ten while Mimi thought.

"It's in the carrier with Gumdrop," Mimi said finally. "I taped it to the bottom of her water dish."

The girls ran to the closet door. Mimi pulled it open.

"Oh my gosh!" Beezel gasped as she looked inside. Someone had torn the closet apart. Their costumes were pulled off their hangers and tossed in all directions. The boxes that held their small props had been dumped upside down and the contents strewn across the floor.

"Gumdrop?" Mimi fell to her knees and began to look through the mess for her snake. Beezel, Hector and Mr. Whaffle quickly searched the other rooms. But Gumdrop and her carrier were gone.

"Someone's taken her!" Mimi said as she looked frantically at Beezel. "My poor little snake! I have to get her back!" She opened the hotel room door and ran down the hall.

"Mimi!" Beezel started after her.

Mr. Whaffle touched her shoulder gently. "I'll go after her," he said. "Poor little thing. She does love that snake."

Beezel closed the door after Mr. Whaffle. She sat down on the sofa. Hector sat down next to her.

"I'm sorry," he said. "I know what that coin means to you both. And what Gumdrop means to our Mimi."

Beezel put her elbows on her knees. She rested her chin on her hands. "It's just that Simon trusted us to take care of it. And now it's gone."

She stood up and walked over to a table next to the closet. She plugged in a small electric kettle they used to make tea in the room. She arranged the teacups neatly on a tray.

"I don't like letting people down," she said. "Especially our circus family."

"Ah, duck," said Hector. "You haven't let anyone down. Things just happen sometimes. That's the way of it."

But Beezel didn't like the "way of it" at all. She wanted to do something to make things right. She had to get the coin back and find Gumdrop. The way Mimi fussed over her snake made Beezel crazy sometimes, but she hated to see her so sad.

By the time the tea was ready, Mr. Whaffle had come back with Mimi. Her eyes were red, but she wasn't crying anymore.

"Gumdrop isn't anywhere," she said. "We looked

up and down the street and in the alley out back. I thought maybe he would leave her there after he took the coin out of her carrier." She shivered.

"I checked at the desk, but the clerk didn't see a thing," Mr. Whaffle said.

"But how did he get into our room?" Mimi asked. "And out of the hotel with Gumdrop?"

"He's a magician, don't forget," said Beezel. "He'd think of a way." She brought the tray over to the coffee table. "Here." She handed a cup to Mimi. "Drink some tea. It'll warm you up."

While they sipped their tea, Beezel and Mimi told Hector about meeting the Great Paparella.

"I bet he took the coin when we went out for lunch," Beezel said. "And that's why I felt like someone was following me. First, he took my change to see if I had Simon's coin with me. And he must have been watching us and seen that Mimi didn't have anything in her pockets. Then he made sure Mr. Whaffle wasn't going to be in our room. He was the one who made that crank phone call."

"But I don't get it," said Mimi. "We can still kapoof. What good is the coin to him? And why did he take poor Gumdrop?" She blew her nose.

"Well . . ." Beezel thought for a minute. "Now that he has the coin, we can't give ka-poofing to anyone else. Maybe that's why he took it. And maybe he took the whole carrier because he was afraid to take Gumdrop out."

"That's silly. Gumdrop wouldn't hurt anyone." She wiped her eyes. "Well, except for a mouse." She took a sip of tea. "Now he wants to have a Magic Duel with us. That can't be good."

"He wants our magic," said Beezel. "But he's not going to get it. We're going to get Simon's coin back." When she thought of Simon and how kind he had been to her, how he had given them the coin, she knew she had to try.

"Well, that does it," Hector said. "My girls are not going to do magic with that evil toad. They most certainly are *not*."

"I agree entirely," said Mr. Whaffle. "It is completely out of the question. We will take this matter up with the authorities." He crossed his arms over his chest.

"But the police might find out about the magic," said Beezel. "Simon wouldn't want that. Think of all the reporters! And the news crews! Then all the evil people in the world would try to get their hands on it. We just *can't* call the police." She looked at Mimi. "Not yet, anyway."

"Beezel's right," Mimi said. "We can still ka-poof. We can think of something, right?"

"Wrong," Mr. Whaffle said. "It's all fine and well to want to keep the Changing Coin a secret, but this is police business."

"But . . . ," said Beezel.

"No way, no how." Hector put his hands on his hips. "Your parents would want us to protect you."

"But . . . ," said Mimi.

"No buts," Mr. Whaffle said. "It's too dangerous."

Beezel looked at Mimi. Mimi looked at Beezel.

"I'll do Mr. Whaffle," said Beezel.

Ka-poof. Mr. Whaffle was a guinea pig. A very unhappy guinea pig. He jumped up and down and chattered up at Beezel.

"He's cute," said Mimi.

"What are you girls up to?" said Hector. "You turn him back this instant!"

"Sorry, Hector," said Mimi.

Ka-poof. Hector was a small white mouse with pink eyes.

Mimi picked him up. "Don't be mad," she said. She slipped him into the large front pocket of her sweatshirt.

"We've just got to find that coin," Beezel said. "It's been a secret for hundreds of years. We can't let people find out about it now. And we *promised* Simon we would give it to a good soul."

"And that slimy creep Paparella sure isn't," said Mimi.

Beezel petted Mr. Whaffle. "It'll be okay. We'll ka-poof you back right after the duel." She picked him up. "You're a very handsome guinea pig, you know."

Mr. Whaffle snorted.

"Now what do we do?" Mimi said. Hector's twitchy nose stuck out of her pocket.

Beezel sighed. It was up to her again. And she had no idea what to do. But they had to do something. She looked at her watch. It was already ten o'clock. They wouldn't get anything done tonight.

Beezel rubbed Mr. Whaffle's ears. She had never seen a guinea pig give someone a dirty look before. But Mr. Whaffle was doing just that. He was glaring at her.

Beezel handed Mr. Whaffle to Mimi and took a

suitcase out of their bedroom closet. She turned it upside down and emptied it on the bed. A deck of cards and her maharajah costume tumbled out.

Mimi set Hector and Mr. Whaffle down inside the open suitcase. "There, that's nice and cozy."

Beezel filled a teacup with water and put it next to them. "And I'll get you an apple," she said.

"Hey, Beezel," Mimi said as she chewed on the ends of her hair. "I've been thinking. What if Paparella won't tell us where the coin is? What if he's gone . . . and the coin's gone, too?"

"I know," said Beezel. What *could* they do if he wouldn't give it back? And if he had left the city, how would they find him? She rubbed her hand across her forehead. "We have to come up with a plan. But first, let's get these little guys some food."

She and Mimi walked out the door of their hotel room in search of mouse and guinea pig snacks. Beezel heard Mr. Whaffle sneeze as she closed the door.

"Bless you," she said.

Mr. Whaffle snorted, as if to say, "Just wait until you ka-poof me back, young lady."

As they walked down to the kitchen, Beezel could

see moonlight streaming through the hotel windows. What was Paparella up to? She sure wished she knew.

Tomorrow night is the Magic Duel, she thought. *And if Paparella shows up, I'm getting our coin back.*

She'd figure out a way. She just had to.

CHAPTER TEN

Beezel and Mimi spent a restless night.

Mimi had a nightmare. She sat straight up and yelled "Paparella!" Then she fell back to sleep.

Beezel thought about Simon, about the last time she had seen him alive. They had been so excited about getting the magic gift that when they left Simon's trailer, they had run all the way home.

Beezel remembered she had tripped, scraping her knee. Mimi ran on ahead, not realizing Beezel had fallen. She sat up and brushed the dirt away. When she looked up, a man was leaning over her.

"Where does Simon Serafin live?" he asked her. Beezel pointed back to his trailer.

"There," she said.

The man had walked off without a word.

Beezel opened her eyes. She hadn't thought about that for a long time. She squinted at the alarm clock. It was 2:30 A.M. She was going to be tired in the morning. She closed her eyes again and said, "I'll try to get your coin back, Simon. I really will. I miss you." Then she fell fast asleep.

When the sun came up at last, both girls were tired and grumpy. Beezel got up first and quietly climbed out of bed.

She peeked down into the suitcase at the foot of the bed. Mr. Whaffle and Hector were curled up against each other, sleeping. "It's time to get some help," she whispered. "And I think I know just the person to call."

She made two phone calls from the sitting room. One call was to the Sleight of Hand Club manager, and one was to an old family friend. When she hung up, she heard Mimi calling her from the bedroom.

"Beezel! Are you up? I'm hungry! Can you get some hot chocolate and toast? After all, you're the one who ka-poofed Mr. Whaffle."

Beezel started to argue and then gave in. It was just easier to get breakfast for her. She took the elevator down to the hotel kitchen. She got a pot of hot chocolate, some toast and another apple for Mr. Whaffle. He had seemed to enjoy the one he had eaten the night before.

Beezel brought the breakfast tray back to their room. They ate together quietly. Mimi looked half asleep, chewing her toast and twirling her hair at the same time. Mr. Whaffle and Hector very politely nibbled on the same piece of toast, one at each end.

"Mimi," Beezel said as she wrote down an address from Mr. Whaffle's notebook, "I've been thinking. There's someone we need to visit today."

"Today?" said Mimi, suddenly wide awake. "Are you crazy? We have to find Gumdrop! We have to get Simon's coin back! We have a show to do! *And* tonight is the Magic Duel!"

"I know," said Beezel. "But this is someone who might be able to help us."

"Who?" said Mimi. She poured some hot chocolate into a saucer for Hector and blew on it to cool it off.

"Meredith," said Beezel.

Mimi stopped. She stared at Beezel as if she had a millipede coming out of her nose.

"Not *the* Meredith?" said Mimi. "Oh no, she

scares me. I'm not going to see her. And you can't make me."

Mr. Whaffle choked on a tiny piece of toast. Beezel tapped him on the back.

"Just listen," said Beezel. "Meredith has known Mom and Dad for years. Mom told me that before she retired from our circus, she was engaged to Mr. Whaffle." She spread some butter on a slice of toast. "Of course that was before he had the accident with the Amazing Aqua Boy. That changed everything. Didn't it, Mr. Whaffle?" Beezel reached down and scratched his back.

"What happened?" asked Mimi.

"He broke up with her. I'm not sure why." Beezel shook her head. "But that's not the point. The point is, she's like family, too. And . . ." She brushed the crumbs off her pants. "Meredith will be able to tell us things no one else can."

Meredith was clairvoyant; a psychic who had visions. She was an expert at reading palms as well. The combination had been irresistible to Mr. Trimoni. He had hired her to be the circus's fortune-teller.

"Well, I'm going," said Beezel. "I called Meredith

this morning. She said she'd love to see us."

"Have a good time," said Mimi.

Beezel looked down at Hector and Mr. Whaffle. Hector was scurrying back and forth. Mr. Whaffle was chattering again. They didn't seem happy.

"Fine," she said to the furry pair in the suitcase. "I'll go by myself." She stood up. "I'm taking the bus. The schedule in the lobby says there's a bus leaving down the street in thirty minutes. Mimi can stay here and take care of you two."

Mimi stuck out her lower lip. "Oh, all right," she said. "But you do the talking. And I'm taking these guys with me. Just in case we need them."

Mimi went to the closet and pulled out a shoe box. She tossed the shoes and the lid on the floor. She picked up the other half of the box and walked to her dresser. After she folded a clean T-shirt and put it inside, she added a piece of toast. Then Mimi tucked the box into the bottom of her backpack.

"In you go," she said as she picked up Mr. Whaffle and Hector and placed them inside. "It's nice and soft in there. And you have a snack. I'll bring some water, too." Mimi grabbed a handful of pens off the floor. She picked up her drawing tablet. "I might as well bring something to do on the bus." She stopped and turned to Beezel. "Do we have enough time to get to Meredith's and back? We have to be back in time for our show. Mr. Whaffle said we're the first act."

Beezel smiled sheepishly at Mimi. "I sort of told a lie," she said. "I called the club manager this morning and told him we're sick."

Mimi stared at her in disbelief. "You did *not*."

Beezel nodded. "But I told him we would do free matinees all next week, to make up for tonight's show. That seemed to make him happy."

Mimi laughed. "You're getting more like me every day."

"I know," Beezel said. "That's what scares me." She rubbed her stomach. "But it's not completely a lie, because my stomach hurts from worrying about the coin and Gumdrop. That counts as being sick, doesn't it?"

Mimi nodded. "And we'll get back in time for the duel?"

"Plenty of time," Beezel said. "But let's go out the back way so the club manager doesn't see us." She took the pens from Mimi. She picked up the pen box from the floor and put the pens inside, one by one, making sure the metal pen tips all faced the same way. Clicking the box shut, she handed it to Mimi and smiled. "Thanks for coming with me."

"What are sisters for?" Mimi said as she put the pen box in the backpack. She sipped the last of her chocolate and slammed the cup down on the tray. "Let's do it," she said.

CHAPTER ELEVEN

Hector was getting carsick. Every time the bus turned a corner, Beezel and Mimi could hear him moan in a small, mouselike way.

"Poor Hector." Mimi reached inside her backpack and picked him up.

"Mimi," whispered Beezel. "Don't hold him up so high. I don't think we're allowed to have mice and guinea pigs on the bus."

"But he's carsick. He should look out the window. That always helps me."

Beezel looked down at the backpack stuck between them on the floor. Mr. Whaffle had climbed halfway out.

"Oh no you don't," said Beezel. She gently pushed him back inside. "You're not carsick. And if we get thrown off, we'll have to *walk* all the way to Meredith's house." She zipped the backpack almost shut, leaving a small opening for air.

The bus pulled into the center of the town where Meredith lived. It wasn't a very big place. Just some stores bordering a main street. No tall buildings like back in the city.

"Come on," Beezel said. Mimi slipped Hector into her pocket and followed her.

Beezel had spent the time on the bus studying a map the desk clerk at the hotel had given her. She knew exactly which way to go.

They came to a street called Bramble Lane. Thorny bushes grew along the fronts of the houses.

As they walked, they checked the addresses on the houses, looking for number 777. They found it at the end, the last house, sitting all alone.

"Oh, sure," said Mimi. "Of course she lives in a haunted house."

"Don't be silly," said Beezel. "It's just old."

Once upon a time it must have been a pretty house, too. Beezel loved the curly carved wood at the corners and eaves. Someday she wanted a house just like it.

There was a black iron gate in front of a small walkway that led to the front door. Mimi gave it a push. The old gate moaned.

"Let's get this over with," she said.

"Yep," said Beezel.

It was so quiet and still that Beezel felt like tiptoeing up the walk. They went up some stairs to the porch. She reached out to knock on the front door.

Just then, it swung wide open. And out stepped Meredith, the fortune-teller. She wore a long blue dress and had stacks of silver and gold bracelets on each arm. Around her head was a red scarf. Long black hair, streaked with gray, spilled out from underneath.

"Come inside. Quickly, girls!" she said as she scanned the walkway behind them. She put one hand behind each of their backs and herded them through the door. "Come in! Come in!"

Beezel was surprised to see her lock the door behind them. "There, that is much better, my dears," Meredith purred. She turned and faced Beezel. Beezel had never seen eyes like hers before. They were a golden amber, just like the color of honey.

She touched Beezel's shoulder and closed her eyes for a moment.

"Hello, Beezel," she said as she opened her eyes.

"Hello," Beezel said.

She turned to Mimi. She touched her hand.

"That makes you Mimi," she said.

"Uh . . . uh . . . ," Mimi stuttered.

Beezel was impressed. How could she know which twin was which? They looked exactly alike. Before Mimi cut her hair, even their parents got mixed up sometimes. And it had been years since Meredith had seen them.

"It has been a long time. Please come, come," she said. Her wrists jangled as she waved them down the hall. "I believe there is something you want to ask me."

They followed Meredith into her living room. She pointed to a red sofa. "Sit, sit," Meredith said. "How can I help you?"

Mimi and Beezel sat next to each other on the sofa. Mimi put the backpack between them. Beezel saw her reach into her pocket and pet Hector nervously.

"It's very hard to explain," Beezel said.

She did her best to tell Meredith about a special coin that had been stolen from them, along with Mimi's snake. But she didn't tell her it was a magic coin: Simon wouldn't have wanted her to do that. She told her they suspected the Great Paparella. And about her parents' trailer getting broken into. But not about the Magic Duel, or the ka-poofing magic.

"If she's a *real* psychic, then she'll know about the Magic Duel," Beezel had said to Mimi on the bus ride there. "If she isn't, then she won't."

Meredith listened carefully to Beezel, then said, "Now let me explain my gift to you. I can't tell my gift how to work. It shows me things, but not always what you are looking for. It can show me the past, the present or the future. Sometimes it shows me nothing at all."

"But you told fortunes in the circus," protested Beezel.

"Yes," she smiled. "I can read palms. But I cannot help everyone." She twirled the end of a long gold necklace around her fingers. "My visions come to me, but not when I call them. Do you understand?"

Beezel nodded. She felt her eyes fill with tears.

"Now, now," Meredith said. "There must be some

way I can help. Do you have something of this Paparella's? An article of clothing? A photograph?"

Beezel reached into the backpack and pulled out the picture from the paper. "Here. This is Paparella."

"Sometimes I get a feeling," said Meredith. She frowned. "Like at the front door just now. I have not felt that way for a long time. For a year after Simon died it was as if something sinister were following me." She glanced down at her hands. "And now it is back." She brushed her hand across her forehead. "Ah, but we have work to do."

Meredith held the picture between her palms. She closed her eyes and was still for a long time.

Mimi leaned over to Beezel and whispered, "Psst! Hey, Beezel! Is she asleep?"

"No," said Meredith. "I am not asleep." She opened her eyes. "This is an evil man," she said quietly. "I think you should be very careful around this man."

"But does he have our coin?" asked Beezel.

"I cannot say for sure," she said. "But I am getting a feeling of foreboding. He is trouble. So maybe yes."

"Will he give it back?" asked Mimi.

"That is more difficult," said Meredith. She took

Mimi's hand and turned it palm side up. "Let me read your palm. Sometimes it helps me see things."

Meredith ran her long polished nail up Mimi's palm. She held her hands. She closed her eyes.

"I'm getting an image . . . ," Meredith said. "You are going to have some sort of battle with Paparella?"

"Yes," said Mimi. "We're supposed to have a magic contest with him. It's called a Magic Duel."

She looked into Mimi's eyes. "You are going to have to give something away. Something that means very much to you, Mimi."

Mimi glanced at Beezel.

"I see you giving up a coin," said Meredith. "A bronze coin. But you told me it had been stolen?" She closed her eyes. "Is this another coin? Ah, wait . . . It is not just the bronze coin you give up . . . It is some kind of gift . . ." Then she sat back in her chair, wide-eyed. She put her hand to her lips. Beezel thought she looked pale.

"Are you okay?" she asked.

"I cannot believe it," Meredith said slowly. "I thought it was a story made up for children. But it's true. You two have the gift. The gift that changes one animal into another."

"Wow!" said Mimi. "See, Beezel? I told you she was amazing!"

Beezel almost said, "You did not!" but she caught herself. Her parents wouldn't want them to argue in front of Meredith. "Yes," she said, smiling through clenched teeth. "I'm sure you did." Were all sisters like this, or was it just hers?

"I heard of this gift," Meredith said, "when I was a little girl."

"Simon gave it to us," said Mimi.

Meredith nodded. "Yes, that makes sense. I knew he had something very special about him."

She tucked a strand of hair back under her scarf. She leaned forward and clasped her hands under her chin. "There is something else that you don't know," she said quietly.

"What?" asked Beezel.

"If the legend is true, yours is not the only coin," said Meredith. "There are two more."

CHAPTER TWELVE

T hree coins!" said Mimi.

"Simon never told us that," said Beezel.

"Maybe he did not know," said Meredith. "Or maybe he did not think it mattered."

"But who has the other coins?" asked Beezel.

"I don't think anyone knows," Meredith said. "Would you like to hear the story?"

"Yes," Beezel and Mimi said together.

Meredith leaned back in her chair. "Long ago, an old magician was nearing the end of his days," she said. "He knew many wondrous and magical things. He knew how to change one animal into another. How to shrink things in size, from big to small, and back again. And he knew how to make people say what they were thinking, just by pointing at them!

"Fearing that his life's work would be lost forever, he discovered a way to keep the magic alive. He forged three bronze coins. On them he printed the words that would bring the magic to life. Each coin had five words. Then he cast a spell. A spell that would keep the magic in the coins as long as the words were never spoken out loud. The only time they could be spoken was when the magic was passed on. Each coin held one of the magician's three secrets.

"The old magician went on a quest to find someone worthy of these gifts. Far away from his home, he found someone. He gave that person the three coins and the secret of how to pass the magic on. And it has been passed down ever since. The spell has never been broken."

Meredith nodded. "My mother swore this story was true. I never believed it. But I saw a bronze coin just now. A coin with five words. And I saw Mimi's gift." Meredith smiled at them. "Mama was right, after all."

"Wow, Beezel," said Mimi. "What if we had all three? We'd be amazing magicians! We could ka-poof and shrink *and* read minds!"

"Mimi," said Beezel, "right now we don't have even one coin. And we just *have* to get it back." She looked at Meredith. "*Do* we get it back?"

Meredith examined Mimi's palm. "Your palm tells me you will have a life-changing event. Maybe that means you will find your coin again. I cannot know this for sure. What I do know is I had two visions. First, I saw you with Paparella, then I saw Mimi giving up your gift. But remember, with my gift, time is shown to me in bits and pieces, like snippets of a movie. However, they are not always in the right order."

"But we wouldn't give up our magic," said Mimi. "Unless it was sometime far in the future. Were we old ladies?"

"I know it was you, Mimi," Meredith said. "How old you were, I do not know."

"I guess we'll be seeing Paparella after all tonight," said Beezel. "We'll just have to think of a plan."

"You should heed my warning about this man," said Meredith. "Do not see him alone. Take Hector and Mr. Whaffle with you."

"Oh, we will," Mimi said, smiling. "Won't we, Beezel?"

"Don't worry about us, Meredith," said Beezel. "We'll be careful. And I'm sorry we didn't tell you the whole truth. But we promised Simon."

"Not to worry," said Meredith as she patted Beezel's shoulder. "I understand promises. It's a good thing to keep them."

Beezel reached into her pocket to give Meredith some money.

"Please." Meredith held her hand in front of Beezel like a stop sign. "You are from the only family I have ever known. The circus. Family doesn't pay."

"Well, then," Beezel said, "will you come see our act? We're at the Sleight of Hand Magic Club in Baltimore for the next two weeks. Would you be our guest one night?"

"I would love to," Meredith said.

"Good," Mimi said. "You can call us at the Destiny Inn."

"We have to go now," Beezel said. She turned to grab the backpack off the sofa. "Oh no!"

Mr. Whaffle was sitting on a sofa cushion, staring up at Meredith. His little mouth was open, and his eyes were moist.

"Oh!" Meredith laughed. "Who is your furry

friend?" She reached down and touched his nose. "You're a cute one. But why so sad?"

Mr. Whaffle closed his mouth and blinked.

Mimi smiled. "That's our guinea pig. He's just tired."

"Ah," said Meredith. "He has such a sweet face for a guinea pig."

"We thought so." Mimi picked up a rather dazed Mr. Whaffle and tucked him inside her sweatshirt pocket next to Hector.

"Good hunting, my dears," Meredith said as she walked them to the door. "I hope to see you soon." She put her hand outside as if she were checking for rain. "It is still there, the gloom I felt before. Get home quickly."

"We will," said Mimi.

"Thank you," said Beezel. The girls turned and ran down the walk.

"And don't forget!" Meredith called after them. "That man, Paparella, he is dangerous! Be very careful!"

CHAPTER THIRTEEN

Beezel shut the gate behind them.

"Do you think Meredith is right?" Mimi asked. "Will Paparella really show up?"

"It makes sense to me," Beezel said. "Because he's not finished with us. The coin won't do him any good unless we give him the words."

Mimi chewed on a strand of hair. She kicked at the sidewalk as she walked. "What do you think he'll do at the duel?"

"I'm not sure," Beezel said. "But at least he can't ka-poof yet." She bent down and picked up a twig. As she walked, she broke off pieces and tossed them into the gutter. She tried to think. How *could* they get the coin back?

Mimi stopped. "Wait a minute," she said. "These

guys keep trying to jump out of my pocket. I'm going to put them in the backpack." She gave Hector and Mr. Whaffle a drink from the water bottle she had brought for them and tucked them inside. "Okay, now it's your turn to carry the backpack." She handed it to Beezel.

"But it's *your* backpack," said Beezel.

"So?" said Mimi. "I carried it here and you should carry it back. That's fair."

Beezel sighed and put on the backpack. She could feel Hector and Mr. Whaffle settling in.

When they got to the bus station, it was midafternoon and several people were waiting. Beezel imagined they were going into Baltimore to have dinner at the harbor, or go to a concert. She would rather be doing anything than confronting the Great Paparella about their missing coin. She had to think of something. And quick.

"Mimi," Beezel said. "About the duel . . . I think we should just ka-poof Paparella the minute we're alone with him."

"How about backstage before it starts?" Mimi suggested.

Beezel nodded. "Then after he's been a snail or a

warthog for a few minutes, we'll ka-poof him back and tell him he has to give us the coin back."

"But what if he won't?" Mimi asked.

"Well, we'll ka-poof him into another animal. Then after a while we'll ka-poof him back again, and ask him once more." She smiled at Mimi. "Nicely, of course. And we'll just keep doing it until he cracks and tells us where the coin is. He can't last forever."

"Yeah, and if he's allergic to ka-poofing like I am, he'll tell us pretty fast."

"Okay, then that's the plan?" Beezel asked.

"Sounds good to me," Mimi said.

Finally, their bus pulled up.

Beezel reached into her pocket and got their return tickets. "We'll have to be very careful when we see him tonight," she said as she got in line to get on the bus. "He's smart, and I'm sure he'll try to trick us. We can't trust him. We'll ka-poof him just as soon as we can. Okay?"

She turned around to Mimi. But Mimi was gone.

"Mimi?" said Beezel. She looked through the crowd. No Mimi. She ran to the ticket booth. She couldn't see her anywhere.

"Mimi!" she called. "Where are you?" Her heart

pounded in her chest. Where was she? Mimi never wandered off without saying something.

"Beezel!"

That's Mimi! thought Beezel. She ran along the street toward the voice. Up ahead, a green car was parked alongside the curb. The door was open. Beezel was sure that Mimi's voice was coming from inside the car.

"Mimi!" she yelled. She ran faster. Mr. Whaffle and Hector bounced against her back. As she was about to reach the car, the door closed. Beezel looked at the back window.

Mimi's face was pressed against it. "Beezel!" Beezel heard her muffled scream as the car sped down the street.

Beezel fell to her knees. Her sides hurt from running. She put her hands over her face. "What am I going to do?" She tried not to cry.

"Are you all right? Did you fall?"

Beezel looked up and saw a young man in a tan delivery uniform.

"You've got to help me," she said. "Someone just kidnapped my sister!"

The man made a phone call at the ticket booth. A

few minutes later two police cars screamed up to the bus stop, lights flashing. A portly man with blotchy skin stepped out of the first car and approached her.

"I'm Officer Dolton," he said. "Are you the young lady that reported a kidnapping?"

"Yes!" said Beezel. "He took my sister!" Beezel took a deep breath. She told him about Mimi being driven away in a green car. About how she suspected the Great Paparella. And that she thought he had stolen a valuable coin from them.

"You've got to find her," she said. "Now!"

"Hold on there a minute," said Officer Dolton. "Let me ask some questions first. What does your sister look like?"

"She's my *identical* twin." Beezel tapped her foot. What was taking him so long?

"Oh, right. Let's take a picture then." He pulled a camera out of the bag he had on his shoulder and took a picture of Beezel. "This will help with our search."

He handed the camera to a man inside the second car. "Steve, run this up to headquarters and get things started. I'll find the girl's parents and see if this isn't some sort of mix-up."

"It's not a mix-up!" said Beezel. "I told you! He took my sister!"

"Let's go see your mom and dad," he said. "And don't you worry. I'll start my men looking right now."

He opened the car door for Beezel. "Which way is home?" he said.

Beezel could feel Mr. Whaffle and Hector scratching inside the backpack. Home? *Now* what was she going to do?

CHAPTER FOURTEEN

On the way back to the hotel, Beezel explained that her parents were on a trip and had left them under the care of their teacher, Mr. Whaffle.

"That's fine," he said. "I'm sure Mr. Whaffle will have a number where I can contact your parents. We'll get this all sorted out. You just try to relax."

Relax? thought Beezel. *Oh, sure. My sister has been kidnapped by a crazy magician. And he has Simon's coin—a magic coin that I promised to take care of. My parents are off in Tibet chasing a yeti. And my family's best friends are in my backpack.* She tried to smile at the officer. He *was* being very kind. But relax? All she wanted to do was cry.

Officer Dolton pulled into the hotel parking lot.

He walked with Beezel to the elevator. On the ride up, Beezel tried to think of a way to explain to him the mess she was in. The elevator door opened and they walked down the hall to her room. She stood in front of the door.

"Don't you have a key?" asked Officer Dolton.

"Oh," Beezel said. "Yeah." She fished for it in her pocket. As she opened the door, a piece of paper fluttered to the ground.

"Someone has left you a letter," said Officer Dolton.

Beezel opened it. It was typed on stationery from the Merlin Hotel. It read:

TONIGHT'S MAGIC DUEL HAS BEEN CANCELED BY THE GREAT PAPARELLA. IF YOU WISH TO RESCHEDULE, PLEASE CALL THE HOTEL.

"Oh my gosh!" said Beezel. "I forgot all about it."

Officer Dolton read the note over her shoulder. "What's the Magic Duel?"

"We were going to have a magic contest with the Great Paparella," Beezel said. "Tonight at midnight. But now he's canceled it."

"Well, let me have that anyway," he said as he took the letter from her, "and we'll check it out."

They stepped into the sitting room.

"So," said Officer Dolton. "Where's Mr. Whaffle?"

"Um," Beezel said. "He might be taking a nap." She pointed to the sofa. "Why don't you sit down and I'll go get him."

"Mind if I use the phone?" he asked.

"Help yourself," said Beezel. Her stomach felt like she had left half of it in the lobby.

She went in the bedroom and closed the door. She took off the backpack and pulled out Hector and Mr. Whaffle. She put them on the bed. Beezel looked back and forth between the angry guinea pig and the sulking white mouse.

She picked up Mr. Whaffle and set him on the floor. "I'm not sure this is going to work," she said to him. "I don't have Mimi near me." Tears filled her eyes. *There's no time for that*, she told herself. *We have to find Mimi.* She quickly wiped them away. "Okay, here goes."

She pointed at Mr. Whaffle. Ka-poof. Mr. Whaffle stood before her. He sputtered. He stammered. Then he took a slow, deep breath.

"Oops," said Beezel. She put her hand to her mouth.

"What on earth were you thinking!" he shouted. "Have you lost your mind entirely? You just wait until I talk to your parents, young lady. And what's this I heard you say about Mimi? Did you say she was *kidnapped*? Why, in all the years I have been with your family . . ."

Beezel stood quietly while Mr. Whaffle let off steam. She had never seen him quite this red in the face. *Almost a cranberry color,* she thought. *But it's just going to get worse. Much worse.*

She pointed to his nose. "Um, Mr. Whaffle . . . ," she said.

"Don't you interrupt me, young lady!"

"But—"

"Just stand still and listen for a change."

Beezel could see it was going to be a long lecture. But she just didn't have the time. Officer Dolton was going to pop in any minute. She had to get his attention.

"Mr. Whaffle!" she tried again.

"I said—" he started.

"Look!" yelled Beezel. She reached up and tapped

him on the nose. "There."

"Ouch!" he said. "What the devil is it *now*?"

"You still have a guinea pig nose," she said quietly.

"What?" Mr. Whaffle froze.

"And paws," she said even more quietly.

Mr. Whaffle walked slowly over to the dresser. He looked in the mirror. He reached up and touched his wet nose with his paw.

"My stars," he said. "I'm only half done."

Just then the door to the bedroom opened.

"Is everything all right in here?" It was Officer Dolton. And he was staring at Mr. Whaffle's nose.

CHAPTER FIFTEEN

Um, Officer Dolton," Beezel said. "This is my teacher, Mr. Whaffle."

Mr. Whaffle held out his paw. "How do you do?"

The officer stepped back. "Wha . . . What are you?" he said.

Mr. Whaffle quickly put both paws in his pants pockets. His nose twitched. He seemed at a loss for words. "I . . . I . . ."

"He's getting ready for our magic act," Beezel said. "He plays the Giant Guinea-Pig Man. Mimi and I change him back." She said it matter-of-factly, hoping it made some sort of sense to him.

"Oh," Officer Dolton said. "No offense, sir. It's just that it looks so real."

"None taken," said Mr. Whaffle. "Now, what's this

about our Mimi being kidnapped?" He puffed up his chest. "And just what are you doing about it?"

Beezel sat down on the bed while Officer Dolton explained how they would search for Mimi. Hector climbed up in her lap and licked her hand. A tear rolled down her cheek and landed on top of Hector's furry head.

I should have known this would happen, she thought. *How stupid can I get? I'm supposed to take care of Mimi. She depends on me.* She picked Hector up and gave him a kiss on his nose. "I'm sorry," she whispered.

Officer Dolton flipped open a notebook and took out a pen. "It's time we called their parents," he said to Mr. Whaffle.

"Yes, of course," said Mr. Whaffle. "Let's all go in the sitting room. My notebook is in there." He pointed with his claw to the notebook lying on the coffee table. "Look under Tibetan Holidays. There's a hotel number listed there. I'd dial the number myself, but my . . . costume . . . makes it difficult."

Officer Dolton opened Mr. Whaffle's notebook and dialed the number.

Beezel listened while Officer Dolton talked to someone on the other end—someone in Tibet. He took his time and patiently explained that Mr. and Mrs. Trimoni had to be contacted at once. But then he frowned.

"I understand," he said. "Well, do the best you can, and we'll call at once if there is any news here on our end."

Officer Dolton hung up the phone. "They can't be reached right now. It seems they're off on an expedition of sorts for the next few days. But the hotel said they would try."

He put his business card next to the phone. "I want you to stay right here," he said. "She might come home, and I'll need you to let me know. Call me at this number." He tapped the card with his finger.

"I keep telling you, Paparella has her," Beezel said. "He's not going to let her go. You have to find him!"

"We'll find him," said Officer Dolton. "And your sister. Try not to worry."

Mr. Whaffle walked the policeman to the door. He closed the door after him and turned to Beezel. "I think it's time we had a little talk," he said.

"I know," said Beezel.

"But first, you ka-poof Hector back this instant," he said.

"But," said Beezel.

"No buts," said Mr. Whaffle.

"Okay." Beezel shrugged. She pointed at Hector. Ka-poof.

"See?" she said.

Hector looked like Hector. Except for the thin white whiskers sticking out from each side of his nose, the two long front teeth that came down over his bottom lip, and the long pink tail that was curled around his feet.

"Squeak," said Hector. "Squeak, squeak."

"Great Aba Daba!" yelled Mr. Whaffle. "Look at what your hocus-pocus has done to poor Hector!"

"Squeak," said Hector. He nodded in agreement.

"I'll fix you just as soon as they find Mimi," Beezel said. "In the meantime, I'll get you some cheese."

Hector crossed his arms and shook his head.

"Let's just have a seat and try not to make things any worse than they are," Mr. Whaffle said as he scratched his nose with his paw, "assuming that's even possible."

Waiting for news about Mimi was awful. Beezel kept opening the door to the hallway and closing it again. She looked over at Mr. Whaffle and Hector.

They're both so mad at me, she thought. *I've never seen them this mad.* She sighed. *And worried.*

The hours passed slowly, and when the phone rang, Beezel almost tripped over Hector in her hurry to answer it.

"Hello?" she said. Beezel looked at Mr. Whaffle. "Oh, hello, Meredith." She tried not to sound disappointed. "It's nice to hear your voice, too."

Mr. Whaffle stood up and walked toward Beezel.

"You saw *what*?" she said into the phone. "You did? You're sure?"

"What's wrong?" Mr. Whaffle said. "Is it about Mimi?"

Beezel nodded. "I will, I'll tell him right now. We will. Thank you. Bye." She hung up the phone.

"What in blazes did she say?" Mr. Whaffle said. "Does she know where Mimi is?"

"No," Beezel said. "But I do. Meredith had one of her visions. At first, she just got this feeling that Mimi was in great danger. Then, all of a sudden, the picture of a three-headed frog came into her head."

Mr. Whaffle took in a long, deep breath and let it out slowly. "Beezel, could you please get to the point? Do you know something about Mimi or *not*?"

Beezel nodded. "I know where she is. She's at the Museum of the Strange and Magical. We saw a three-headed frog in a jar there." She touched Mr. Whaffle's arm. "We have to call the police right now. We have to go get her. Meredith said she's in terrible trouble."

Mr. Whaffle began to pace. "Terrible trouble?" he mumbled. "And Meredith saw this frog?" He pointed his claw at Beezel. "She's never been wrong, you know. Never once got a vision wrong." He stopped pacing. "We're calling Officer Dolton right now."

Hector dialed the number and held the phone to Mr. Whaffle's ear.

"Officer Dolton?" he said. "Mr. Whaffle here. We know where Mimi is. She's at the Museum of the Strange and Magical. How do I know? Well, we've had a vision. Well, of course *we* didn't have one, our friend Meredith did. She called and told us about it." There was a pause. "No, no, she had nothing to do with the kidnapping, I'm quite sure of that. You see, she used to be our fortune-teller in the Trimoni Circus, and she has these little visions now and then. She even knew I was going to pierce the Amazing Aqua Boy's flipper. But I wouldn't listen to her. Just being stubborn, I guess. But now she's had a vision about Mimi. She saw danger and a three-headed frog and our Mimi and . . ."

Mr. Whaffle moved his head away from the phone. Beezel could hear Officer Dolton yelling.

"I assure you this is *not* a joke," Mr. Whaffle said. "Meredith is quite a talented psychic and fortune-teller. So if she said she saw a three-headed frog, you can rest assured she did." There was another pause. "Well, you don't have to be insulting about it. I understand. Yes. Well, good-bye." Hector hung up the phone for Mr. Whaffle.

"What did he say?" Beezel asked. Mr. Whaffle looked more than a little angry.

"He said"—Mr. Whaffle cleared his throat—"either I was pulling some sort of tasteless prank or the stress was getting to me. He said he thought I should take an aspirin and lie down."

Beezel watched as his cheeks turned that bright cranberry color again.

Hector looked agitated as well. "Squeak, squeak," he said, shaking his fist at the phone.

"I quite agree, Hector." Mr. Whaffle's voice was a little louder. "He had the nerve to say that psychics and three-headed frogs would just have to wait until after he was finished with all his 'legitimate' leads. *Then* he'd run by the museum and check things out." Mr. Whaffle put his paws on his hips. "Of all the nerve . . . ," he started.

"Let's go without him," Beezel interrupted. "It's getting late. I can't stand the thought of Mimi being in that museum with Paparella a minute longer." She grabbed her sweater and yanked it on. "And Meredith said Mimi was in danger."

Hector nodded in agreement.

"We'll get a cab out front," Mr. Whaffle said. He tried to pick up his wallet and room key from the coffee table. "Would you mind, Hector? It's these darn paws." Hector nodded and picked them up for him.

"We can make a plan on the way over," Mr. Whaffle said as he turned and faced Beezel. "Speaking of which, you've gotten us into enough trouble today. So the only people in this room allowed to have plans from now on are Hector and me. Is that clear?"

Beezel looked at them. Mr. Whaffle's face was still red. Hector looked as disgusted with her as any mouse-man could.

"Clear," she said.

Beezel followed Hector and Mr. Whaffle out of the room.

"Lock the door behind you," Mr. Whaffle said.

Beezel waited until they were a little way down the hall, then dashed back inside the room. She picked up Gadget's cage and eyed the tarantula inside. "You're coming with me, Gadget," she said as she shoved the cage in Mimi's backpack and slipped it on.

She locked the door behind her. "Because, whether they like it or not, I *do* have a plan."

CHAPTER SIXTEEN

Beezel ran down the stairs after Mr. Whaffle and Hector. They dashed across the lobby. Several people stopped to stare and point at Mr. Whaffle's nose and Hector's long pink tail. When they got to the curb, Mr. Whaffle waved his paw. A taxi pulled up alongside them.

"Hop in," he said to Hector and Beezel. "We've no time to lose."

Beezel sat in the backseat between them.

"Where to?" asked the cabdriver as he looked in his rearview mirror. "Costume party tonight?"

"The Museum of the Strange and Magical," Beezel said.

"Sweetheart, that place isn't open this time of night," the driver said.

"Sir, we did not ask the hours," Mr. Whaffle said, waving a paw at the driver. "Just take us there."

"Geez, someone's cranky," the driver muttered.

While Mr. Whaffle spoke to Hector in low tones about what he would do to Paparella once he got his paws on him, Beezel struggled with how to get them to go along with her idea.

They're both so mad at me, they're not going to listen to anything I have to say, she thought. Maybe she could let them think they had come up with the idea themselves. Maybe that would work.

The cab pulled up in front of the museum. Hector handed the driver some money from Mr. Whaffle's wallet. Beezel waited until the taxi pulled away before she tried to open the front door.

"Stardust and spangles," she muttered. "It's locked." She knelt down and looked under the door. "Gee, you'd have to be pretty small to fit under there." She looked up at Hector innocently.

Hector scratched his head in thought. He pointed to his chest and then to the bottom of the door. "Squeak."

"You, Hector?" Mr. Whaffle said. "Oh, I don't know. Remember what happened the last time she ka-poofed us." He held out his paws.

Beezel stood up and brushed off her pants. She had to be careful how she said things. "You're right," she said. "It's too risky—even though I could fix everything as soon as I got close to Mimi and our magic was working again." She shook her head. "No, there has to be another way."

Mr. Whaffle scratched his chin with one claw. "You sure you want her to ka-poof you back into a mouse, Hector?"

Hector nodded.

Beezel didn't waste any time. She pointed to Hector. Ka-poof. Hector was a mouse.

"At least you're a *normal* mouse," Beezel said. "Well, except for the long white hair on top of your head. And you don't seem to have a tail."

"Well, I don't feel normal," Hector said in a tiny mouse voice. "Not at all. Except for my teeth." He flashed a wide grin at Beezel. "See?" Hector had a mouth full of little human teeth.

"Heavens to mergatroid!" said Mr. Whaffle. "Now he's a *talking* mouse!"

"Oh dear," Beezel said. "I'm so sorry, Hector. I'll fix you as soon as I can." She picked him up and placed him by the bottom of the door. "See if you can slip underneath and unlock it somehow."

"Okay, I'll try," he squeaked. "But I hope they don't have any mousetraps in there."

"Wait," she said. "Take this." She unfastened a clip from the end of her braid. "This might help. Maybe you can use the metal part to pick the lock."

He nodded. "I can hold it with my teeth. Pass it under the door when I get in."

Hector squeezed under the door.

"He's in," Beezel said as she pushed the hair clip in after him.

She heard a small commotion at the doorknob. Hector's high-pitched grumbling wafted through the keyhole. And finally Beezel heard a click.

"Try it now," Hector called.

Beezel turned the knob and slowly opened the door. Hector sat on the polished tile floor of the museum. He was grinning from ear to ear.

"Feeling pretty proud of yourself, aren't you?" said Beezel as she picked him up.

"Indeed, I am," he squeaked.

"Good job, Hector," Mr. Whaffle said. "Now ka-poof him back and let's go find Mimi."

Beezel scratched Hector's ears and sighed. "It's too bad we aren't invisible. You know, so we could sneak around the halls and find out what room Mimi is in. We're so big, we'll have to be careful not to make any noise." She looked out the corner of her eye at Mr. Whaffle. "He might hurt Mimi or get away."

"Hmm," Mr. Whaffle said. "I've been thinking. What if you ka-poof me into a mouse as well? And leave Hector as he is? Then we can check the rooms on each floor . . ."

"Then come get me when you find out where she is, I can ka-poof you both back, and we'll rescue Mimi!" Beezel finished for him. "I think that's a brilliant plan, Mr. Whaffle, don't you, Hector?"

"Just the ticket," Hector said. "And it will keep you safe . . ."

"Because," Beezel interrupted, "I'll be hiding, waiting for you, and I'll only come out when you find her! Good thinking, Hector!"

Hector smiled. "Just using the old noggin."

Mr. Whaffle rubbed his paw across his forehead. "At least with our plan you'll be out of harm's way." He looked down at Hector. "And we can move around the museum without being seen or heard."

"Quiet as a mouse," Hector agreed.

"So I'll ka-poof you into . . . a . . . mouse." Beezel looked up at Mr. Whaffle's face. He already had parts of one animal on him. What if she ka-poofed him into a mouse, and he ended up with mouse, human *and* guinea pig parts?

It seemed to Beezel that Mr. Whaffle was thinking the same thing, because he said, "I think it might be wise to just change me back into a guinea pig. Less complicated. But first, promise me you'll change us back as soon as we get close to Mimi. Then we'll call the police and tell Dolton we've found her."

"I promise," Beezel said.

Mr. Whaffle stared deeply into her eyes. "Do you circus swear?" he said as he held out his paw.

Everyone in the Trimoni camp knew a circus swear was pretty serious. "I swear," she said as she took his paw and shook it, "on P. T. Barnum's ghost."

Mr. Whaffle seemed to relax a little after hearing Beezel make her promise. "Let's get on with it, then," he said.

Beezel pointed at him. Ka-poof. "Uh oh," she said

as she picked him up. Now he was a guinea pig with a tiny human nose and tiny human hands.

"Don't worry, Mr. Whaffle," Beezel said. "You won't be like this for long." She held Hector and Mr. Whaffle, one in each hand, and entered the museum. Beezel tiptoed past the lobby and the gift shop. As she entered the main hallway, she noticed that all the doors to the display rooms were shut.

"I'm going to put you down now," Beezel whispered. "Take a quick peek under the doors and come right back. I'll wait here."

Mr. Whaffle tapped Hector on the back. He pointed to the left side of the hallway.

"Roger that," squeaked Hector. "I'll check the rooms on the left." He scampered down the hall.

Mr. Whaffle looked up at Beezel. She touched him on the top of his head. "I'll be fine. I'll hide in the Cabinets of Wonder." She pointed to the room that held the jar with the three-headed frog. There was no door to that room, just a rope swag hung across the entrance. Mr. Whaffle scampered underneath it, and after checking the room, nodded his approval. Then he turned and ran down the right side of the main hall.

A strange green glow came from the lights behind the shelves that held all the jars. Beezel unhooked the rope swag and went inside. She found a small nook to hide in between two large glass cases. She crawled in, slipped off the backpack and took out Gadget's cage. She whispered to the tarantula, "You're my insurance, you know. You're going to help me test my magic and let me know when we're getting close to Mimi."

Beezel opened the cage and looked inside. "Let's see. You'll need to be small enough to fit in your cage. And you can't have wings or you might fly away. How about a little lizard?"

She pointed at the spider. Ka-poof.

"Oh dear," whispered Beezel. Gadget still had all her legs, and even her spider eyes. But now she had a lizard's tail.

Beezel quickly closed the top of the cage. "We'll try again in a minute." She put Gadget's cage back inside the backpack and waited. After a few minutes passed, Mr. Whaffle and Hector scurried up to her.

"We don't see her anywhere on this floor," Hector said.

Mr. Whaffle nodded in agreement.

"Then let's go up one flight." Beezel picked up Mr. Whaffle and Hector and put one in each of her sweater pockets. She dashed up the stairs and set Hector and Mr. Whaffle down in the hallway.

"Be careful," she whispered as she watched them scamper down the hall.

While she waited, Beezel tested Gadget again. This time the spider looked a little bit more like a lizard. She had eight hairy spider legs, but she had a lizard's head and tail.

"This is great! We're getting closer," she whispered to Gadget excitedly. "I bet Mimi is somewhere on this floor."

She sat by the open stairwell door and waited impatiently for Mr. Whaffle and Hector to return. *Where are they?* Beezel wondered. She couldn't stand to wait much longer, knowing that Mimi was somewhere nearby. *Maybe I'll just sneak down the hall and try to figure out which room Mimi is in,* she thought. *And if I see Paparella, I'll just ka-poof him into something.*

Beezel quietly opened the door and crept out into the hall. She squinted in the darkness, trying to spot Hector or Mr. Whaffle. But she saw nothing. She crawled over to the first room on the left side of the hall and tested Gadget. There were no changes. She had the head and tail of a lizard, but the rest of her was still spider.

Beezel crossed the hall and tested Gadget at the door of the first room on the right. She was the same as before—there were no new lizard parts. She tried the second room on each side of the hallway. No changes there either.

Maybe Mr. Whaffle and Hector have already found her, Beezel thought hopefully. She knelt in front of the third door on the right. *I'll just do one more test, then go back and wait for them.*

Beezel pointed at Gadget. Ka-poof. She was a lizard. Ka-poof. She was a spider.

Her magic worked perfectly! Mimi had to be inside that room! But now what should she do? Should she find Hector and Mr. Whaffle? What if Paparella did something to Mimi while she looked for them? Maybe she should go inside and ka-poof him before he could. She stood up and put her hand on the doorknob.

But then Beezel remembered her promise to Mr. Whaffle. She had never broken a circus promise in her life. She pulled her hand away.

I'll find Mr. Whaffle and Hector first, she thought to herself. *I'll ka-poof them back to normal, right here in front of this room. Then we'll go inside together and get Mimi.* Beezel leaned over to pick up Gadget's cage.

That's when someone reached around her from behind and grabbed both of her hands.

CHAPTER SEVENTEEN

Can't have you pointing at me, now, can I?"
Paparella said as he stood carefully to her side. He
tied Beezel's wrists together with a rope.

"Help!" she screamed.

Paparella took a second rope and tied her arms
against her stomach. "There's no one here to help
you," he said as he opened the door. "Come inside.
I wasn't planning on picking you up until later
tonight. But this works out fine. We'll do this now
and get it over with."

He shut the door behind them and locked it.
He flipped on a light switch. A neon sign flickered
on. ELECTRICITY AND MAGIC flashed in orange and
green.

The room was full of all sorts of strange devices.

In the center of the room was Mimi, strapped into what looked like an electric chair.

Beezel ran to Mimi. "Are you okay?"

"I'm sorry, Beezel," said Mimi. "He had Gumdrop. He said he would kill her if I didn't get in the car. I thought I could ka-poof him and rescue her. But he grabbed my hands right away. He is *really* fast."

"It'll be okay, Mimi," she said. "Don't worry." She turned and faced Paparella. "Let her go!" Beezel tried to free her hands, but Paparella had done a good job of tying them. "Take those straps off of her! You're going to go to jail for this! You can't kidnap people—"

"And poor innocent snakes!" interrupted Mimi.

"—and steal things and break into museums!" Beezel finished.

"Oh, I wouldn't say I *broke* in," Paparella said. "My apartment is directly above the museum. I can crawl through a window in the Telepathic Theater anytime I wish. Finkleroy is never very good about locking it."

He ran his hand over the arm of the electric chair. "And as for the rest of it, what can I say?

Today has been my lucky day. I was looking for the coin in your closet when I accidentally tripped over *that*."

Paparella pointed to the floor next to the electric chair where Gumdrop was curled up in her carrier.

"I saw the coin taped to her dish, and then, bingo! I had an idea. I knew how to get the magic from the two of you." He smiled at Beezel. "You would do anything for your sister . . ." He glanced at Mimi. "And your sister would do anything for that snake."

Paparella tapped the side of Gumdrop's carrier with the tip of his boot. The big snake hissed.

"Don't do that!" yelled Mimi. "It scares her!"

Paparella chuckled. "You're a feisty one. You would dearly love to turn me into something squishable, wouldn't you? So I have to be very careful. Especially with the two of you together. The magic is at full strength again, isn't it?"

Beezel turned to Mimi. "Did you tell him about the magic?"

"He already knew," said Mimi. "He knew all about it."

"But how did you find out?" Beezel asked Paparella.

"I learned from the same person Simon did." Paparella shot her such a hateful look that Beezel shuddered. "But it should have been mine in the first place. It was *my* birthright!" he hissed. "However, our mother did not agree."

Beezel looked at him in disbelief. "You can't be," she said. "You're Simon's *brother*?"

"Yes," said Paparella. "I was Peter Serafin, Simon's older brother. But I gave up my family when my mother gave the Changing Coin to Simon instead of me." He pounded his chest with his fist. "Her *eldest* son. I am no longer a Serafin."

Paparella then took an empty chair and pulled it over. He turned it to face Mimi. He grabbed Beezel by the shoulders and shoved her down in it.

With one hand, Paparella undid the rope that held her hands against her waist.

Beezel tried to raise her wrists and point at him, but Paparella's other hand held them firmly away.

He's as strong as Simon, she thought.

He took the rope and lashed her bound hands to

the arm of the electric chair, right next to Mimi's strapped hand. The sides of their hands touched. "There," he said. "That should do nicely."

"You're a horrible person," said Mimi. "You're nothing like Simon. You didn't deserve the coin."

"Oh, please," said Paparella. "Spare me. Simon was just like my mother." He stared at his hands. "One day I saw them walk into a field together. I had a feeling she was up to something. So I followed them and hid behind some bushes. I heard her tell him all about the coin—its power and its rules." He smirked. "Then before I could stop her, she pressed the coin into Simon's hand and whispered the words into his ear. Just like that." He snapped his fingers. "She was fast, too." He leaned over Mimi and tightened a strap. "At least I inherited *that* from her."

Beezel pulled hard against the rope that held her hands to the chair. It wouldn't budge. *What am I going to do? Where are Mr. Whaffle and Hector?* she thought. But what good would a mouse and a guinea pig be against Paparella? Officer Dolton said he would come by the museum tonight. But what if he was too late? She had to do something. Maybe she could keep him talking.

"Simon would never have told you *we* had the gift," Beezel said. "How did you find out?"

Paparella chuckled. "Yes, that part is amusing. I was sure Simon had given the coin to that fortune-teller. She acted so oddly, as if she knew someone was watching her. I figured she had something to hide. So I followed her for months, waiting for a sign that she had the power."

"Meredith?" said Beezel. So that was the bad feeling that had followed her for a year.

"Yes," he said. "But it was a complete waste of my time. After that, I had no idea who had the coin. So I perfected my magic and kept my eye on the Trimoni Circus. Imagine my delight when I heard that the Trimoni Twins were performing the Changing Illusion. Of course, it would have been much easier if Simon had just told me. I could have grabbed you both on the day he died."

"The mark on your face!" said Beezel. Now she remembered where she had seen it before. On the day they got the gift from Simon. It was Paparella who had leaned down to ask her where he lived.

"Yes," Paparella said. "My village has a quaint custom. They mark the people they think are evil with a sign. To protect all the good law-abiding citizens." He reached up and touched his cheek. "They did this right before they banished me."

Beezel watched as he stood behind the electric chair.

"Now, about this contraption," he said, as he leaned against it. "I've been doing some tinkering after hours, and I've improved this device considerably. When I push this little button"—he pointed to a button on the side of the chair—"the power booster I've attached sends thousands of volts through the chair." He smiled happily. "It's now capable of turning a Brahma bull into a pile of crisp beef jerky."

Beezel felt the anger building up inside her. "It's just a phony electric chair," she said. "This museum is full of tricks."

"So you think it's a trick?" he said. "Well, then, let's try it, shall we?" He put his finger on the button.

"Beezel!" Mimi yelled. "Believe me, it's not a trick. He showed me how it works."

"Yes," said Paparella. "It gives new meaning to the term 'well done.'" He smiled at her. "Now, let's get on with it. And please be good little girls. I'd hate to push that button."

Beezel felt something crawl up her leg. Next she felt a tugging on her wrists, as if someone underneath the arm of the chair were pulling on the ropes that held her. Then a small furry ball nestled against her neck.

"Mr. Whaffle will have you undone in a flash," Hector whispered into Beezel's ear in his tiny mouse voice. "He's almost chewed his way through the ropes. He'll tap you when he's finished. I've got to get something out of the backpack." He scurried down the back of her neck.

Beezel could feel Mr. Whaffle struggling with the rope that held her arms to the chair. Maybe he had already gnawed through them. But she hadn't felt a tap. *I have to keep Paparella talking,* she thought. Her voice came out more like a whisper. "After we give you the gift, you'll let us go?"

"But of course I will," Paparella said as he fussed with some wires that were attached to the metal cap over Mimi's head.

Beezel knew he was lying. He was going to get rid of both of them just as soon as he could. She didn't care about the coin anymore. She just wanted to save Mimi. But how?

She thought about Meredith's prediction. If they gave Paparella the gift, he would probably ka-poof them into slugs and stomp on them with his boots. But Meredith had said Mimi would have to give up her gift.

An idea popped into Beezel's head. *Meredith was talking to Mimi the whole time. It was Mimi's palm she read. Meredith didn't say anything about me giving up anything.* Maybe Beezel could keep her half of the gift. Just long enough to save Mimi somehow.

"There," Paparella said. "We just need one more thing." He put his right hand in his pocket and pulled out the coin. Beezel's throat tightened. Why hadn't Mr. Whaffle tapped her yet?

"Don't try to trick me. I know the five words. Say them exactly the way they are written here," Paparella said, pointing to the words on the coin. "*Both* of you." He laid the coin on top of where the twins' hands touched. Beezel could feel Mimi's fingers trembling against hers.

Paparella laid his right hand on top of the coin. His hand was so large it covered both of theirs. Beezel felt his sweaty palm resting against her hand.

"Do it," he said. "Or I will push the button. I promise you. If I can't have the gift, you two certainly won't. Besides, the coin alone is worth a fortune. So I win either way." He kept his left hand on the button.

Beezel felt a strong tapping on the bottom of her forearm. She took a deep breath and looked at her sister. "We have to give him the gift, Mimi. We have no other choice."

Mimi nodded.

Beezel and Mimi said the first word. They said the second. The third.

Beezel watched Paparella closely. He stared intently at his right hand. She had to be careful and look for an opportunity. If he sensed she was going to move her hand away, it would all be over.

But maybe there would be time if she was fast. Faster than Paparella. And if she was right about being able to keep her half of the magic.

The twins said the fourth word. As they began to say the fifth and final magic word, Paparella glanced over at Mimi and smiled.

Beezel knew this was her only chance. She stopped speaking in midword.

CHAPTER EIGHTEEN

Beezel yanked her hands away a split second before Mimi finished saying the fifth word alone. Only Mimi's hand was left under Paparella's.

Please let me still have my half of the magic! Beezel thought.

She had been able to pull her hands away from Mimi's, but one rope was still caught around the arm of the chair. Beezel pulled at it frantically as she struggled to raise her arms high enough to point at Paparella.

Paparella quickly pushed the button with one hand and grabbed Simon's coin with the other. "I warned you!"

Beezel heard the power booster click on. "No!" she screamed. She gave one final yank and the last rope around her hands fell to the floor. She thought the five words faster than she ever had in her life and pointed at Mimi.

Ka-poof. Mimi was a bat. She slipped out from under the straps and flew away. The straps crackled and sparked as they fell back against the chair.

Mimi wasn't just a bat, she was a terrified bat. Beezel tried to point at Paparella, but Mimi flapped back and forth in front of her.

"Mimi!" Beezel said as she stood up. "You're okay! Get out of the way!" She tried to wave Mimi away.

Paparella ducked behind the electric chair. "Let's see if I got your sister's half!" he said as he quickly leaned out from behind the chair, raised his hand and pointed at Beezel's head—right as Mimi swooped in front of her.

Ka-poof.

Beezel stared open-mouthed at the enormous creature that was standing on its hind legs in front of her. It looked just like a pig, except that sticking out of its shoulders was a pair of flapping bat wings.

"Mimi?" Beezel said. What had happened? *The magic must have gotten messed up somehow,* she thought. *Maybe Paparella got just a little bit of it.*

"Oink! Oink!" Mimi cried in a complete panic. She tried to scratch her stomach with her front hooves.

Before Beezel could raise her hand to ka-poof her back, Mimi lost her balance and lurched toward her, knocking her flat. She fell across Beezel's chest, pinning her to the floor like an enormous pink paperweight.

"Snort!" cried Mimi. "Snort!"

"Mimi! Get off of me!" wheezed Beezel, gasping for air. "I know you must be itching like crazy, but if you don't get off me right now, you're going to be a bat-pig forever!" But Mimi wasn't listening. She just squealed, snorted and flapped her wings.

Beezel's right arm was completely trapped under Mimi's fat stomach. She pulled and pulled, but it wouldn't budge. She tried her left arm. She could move it only a little bit.

Paparella came out from behind the chair. "Well, now," he chuckled. "This is fine, just fine. I do believe I'm going to have the last laugh after all." He looked down at Beezel. "Either give me your half, or I'll change you into something you'll regret. If you think bat-pig here is strange"—he looked at Mimi and winced—"wait until you see what I am going to do to you! You'll be worm-girl, and then your fat sister will crush you flat. I'll give you exactly ten seconds to think it over. One, two, three . . ."

I'm going to be a worm in just a few more seconds if I don't get her off me, Beezel thought as Paparella counted. *And of course, then Mimi will squish me flat. She won't mean to, she just will.*

"Mimi, get off!" Beezel pulled her left arm with all her might.

"Ten," Paparella said. "Time's up. But you know what? I think I'll keep your sister just like she is. She'll make me a ton of money in a sideshow." He laughed. "Well, here goes." He started to raise his hand to point at Beezel.

She heard a whirring sound.

Phffft!

The Great Paparella grabbed his right hand in pain. Simon's coin went spinning to the ground.

"Arrgh!" he screamed. "Who did that?"

One of Mimi's art pens was stuck through the middle of Paparella's palm.

Phffft! Another pen flew threw the air. This one

struck the Great Paparella in his shoulder.

Beezel turned her head to see who had come to her rescue. Standing on the arm of the chair Beezel had been sitting in was a very angry and determined guinea pig. And right next to him, propping Mimi's pen box open with his two paws, was Hector. Mr. Whaffle reached down into the box with his tiny human hands and snatched up the next pen in the set.

Phffft! The Great Paparella had a pen stuck in his rear end.

"Nice shot that was, Mr. Whaffle!" squeaked Hector.

"Arrgh!" Paparella tried to kick the chair.

But Mr. Whaffle was much too quick.

Phffft! Phffft! Phffft! Phffft! Mr. Whaffle hurled two pens into each of Paparella's boots.

"Ouch! Stop that!" Paparella said as he danced around the room. "These are made from fine Italian leather!"

Beezel tried as hard as she could to pull her left arm out. It wouldn't budge.

"Mimi, listen to me!" It was getting harder to breathe. "Get off me so I can ka-poof you. Then you won't itch! And hurry up!"

Mimi slowly moved off of Beezel. Beezel's right arm was completely numb. She sat up and tried to raise her left hand to point at Paparella. At the same time, the Great Paparella was trying to point his left hand at her.

"Oh no!" Beezel cried.

But then, like a furry white arrow, Hector shot down the chair and across the floor. "Ah yaaaa!" he screamed. He flew straight up the side of the Great Paparella. And he bit him. Hard. On the index finger of his left hand.

"Arrgh!" the Great Paparella screamed.

He waved Hector back and forth like a flag. But Hector held on tight.

Mimi pushed against Beezel's back.

"Okay, Mimi," Beezel said. "Let's fix you. Hector's keeping Paparella busy." She pointed to Mimi.

Ka-poof. Mimi was Mimi again. Her pig body and bat wings were gone.

"Are you okay?" asked Beezel. She reached over and grabbed Simon's coin from the floor. She shoved it down into her pants pocket.

Mimi quickly felt her nose, stomach, arms and

legs. "I'm still a little itchy," she said. "But it'll wear off. I feel *so* much better."

They looked at Paparella. Mr. Whaffle was just about finished with the art pens. Several were stuck in Paparella's backside. The Great Paparella jumped up and down like a crazed porcupine.

"Beezel, now!" Mimi said. "Ka-poof him!"

"Okay, here goes." Beezel tried to point at Paparella. "But it's hard to hit a moving target."

Ka-poof. Hector was a three-toed sloth. But he didn't stop biting Paparella. He held on for all he was worth. Paparella couldn't wave him around anymore. Now he was just trying to pull him off.

"Oops!" Beezel pointed again. Ka-poof. The Great Paparella was a fat toad. She pointed to Hector. Ka-poof. Hector was human again.

Hector grimaced and pulled Paparella the toad out of his mouth. He looked at it in disgust and dropped the toad on the floor.

"Blech," Hector said. "That leaves an awful taste in your mouth."

Mimi reached down and picked up the toad. "Good choice, Beez." Mimi put Paparella in her backpack and zipped it shut.

"Thanks!" Beezel said as she pointed to Mr. Whaffle.

Ka-poof. He was back to normal. No guinea pig parts. A human nose and human hands.

"Ah-choo!" Mr. Whaffle sneezed.

"Bless you," said Mimi.

"Mr. Whaffle!" said Beezel. "Thank you!" She ran and hugged his wide belly. "And you, too, Hector. For saving us. I'm sorry we ka-poofed you."

"Yeah," said Mimi. "I hope I never get ka-poofed again. Even my teeth were itchy." She ran to Gumdrop's carrier, picked up the big snake and gave it a kiss. "You okay, sweetie?"

"Mr. Whaffle," Beezel said, "I'm sorry I didn't listen to you. We should have called the police right after the coin was taken."

"I should be furious with the two of you," Mr. Whaffle said as he unplugged the electric chair.

"Furious," said Hector.

"I should give you the lecture of your young lives," said Mr. Whaffle.

"A good long lecture!" Hector nodded vigorously.

Mimi pulled the watch out of her sleeve. She held it up. She started to swing it back and forth.

"*But* . . . " Mr. Whaffle reached over and stopped the watch from swinging. He plucked it from Mimi's hand and put it in his jacket pocket. "I suppose all's well that ends well."

"And the coin *is* safe again," said Hector.

Mr. Whaffle brushed the sleeves of his jacket. "Thank goodness Hector and I had time to run inside here before Paparella shut that door." He looked at Beezel. "And I was certainly glad to have my hands. I would never have been able to throw pens with paws."

"Thanks for not getting too mad," said Beezel. "I promise it won't happen again."

"Be careful what you promise, my sweet," said Hector. "I know how life can be with you two girls. Up and down, down and up. Who knows what could happen next? You could change me into a hyena . . . or a magpie . . . or . . ."

"But," Mimi interrupted, "*now* what are we going to do? If we ka-poof Paparella back to normal, he'll try to ka-poof Beezel into something horrible. And if he does, we're all going to be toads." She rubbed her forehead with her hand. "Or even worse than toads. Toad-people! It makes my head hurt."

Beezel stood quietly for a while. She was thinking about the magic. Maybe the magic was like an electric current, and when it started to leave them, and she pulled her hand away, Paparella got only a diluted version, just a little bit that flowed out from Mimi to him.

Simon was right, she thought. *We have to figure out how the magic works with twins all by ourselves.*

"Mimi," she said, "do you have *any* of your magic left?"

Mimi pointed at Hector. Nothing happened. "Nope."

"Excuse me!" Hector said in exasperation. "Wasn't it *you* who said you'd never ka-poof me again? And here you are, not one minute later, trying to turn poor old Hector into another one of your lab experiments."

"That was Beezel." Mimi smiled innocently. "*I* didn't promise anything."

Beezel scratched the back of her neck. It was a puzzle. Normally, she liked puzzles. There had to be some way to get the magic back from Paparella. Keeping him as a small and helpless animal was a good idea. That way he couldn't ka-poof them or run away. But how could he give them back the magic? She put her hands on her hips. She tapped her foot. Then she looked at Mimi.

"Hey," said Beezel as a big smile began to spread across her face. "I have an idea."

CHAPTER NINETEEN

Beezel took Paparella out of the backpack and set him on the floor. "Watch this."

Ka-poof. The Great Paparella was a mynah bird.

"A mynah bird? But what good will that do us?" Mimi said as she twirled her hair. "Oh, wait!" She smiled at Beezel. "I get it."

Hector said, "Are you doing what I *think* you're doing?"

Mr. Whaffle bristled. "Could everyone please just *say* what they mean?"

Beezel ignored both Hector and Mr. Whaffle. "Let's see if it worked," she said to Mimi.

Beezel knelt down next to the mynah. "Hello, there, Mr. Paparella. Are you ready to give Mimi back her magic yet?"

The mynah bird snapped its beak in Beezel's face. "The magic is mine!" he said in a high-pitched bird voice. "*And* the coin. You'll have to do better than this." He flapped his wings and tried to fly.

"You're not going to get very far flying," Beezel said. "After all, I can ka-poof you into a snail mid-flight. Snails can't fly."

"Rotten kid," muttered the mynah as he closed his wings.

Beezel nodded her head at the mynah with satisfaction. "This is perfect. He *can* talk. He's a bird, but he's still Paparella. So he can say the magic words to us."

"But he said he won't do it," Mimi said.

"Then we'll help him change his mind," Beezel said. She whispered something in Mimi's ear.

Mimi laughed. "Good one, Beez." She pulled Gumdrop's carrier next to Paparella.

"What?" squawked Paparella the mynah as he eyed the girls. "What are you dreadful children up to now?"

Mimi took Gumdrop off her shoulders and

gently put her down inside her carrier. "It's dinner time," she told her snake.

"What are you trying to do?" the mynah asked. "Scare me? It won't work. I know you wouldn't feed a defenseless bird to that hideous snake."

"Of course we won't," Beezel said.

"Your beak would give her indigestion," Mimi agreed.

Beezel pointed to the mynah. Ka-poof. Paparella was a small gray mouse. She reached over and picked him up by the tail.

"In you go!" Mimi called happily. "And Gumdrop will be thrilled to see you. She hasn't had a mouse in a week. Poor thing, she's probably starving."

"He's so little, he's really just an appetizer," Beezel said as she dropped Paparella into Gumdrop's carrier.

The big snake's tongue flicked in and out. "She knows you're in there with her, Mr. Paparella," Mimi said. "And she remembers how you treated her. It won't be long now."

Beezel looked down at Paparella and Gumdrop. The big snake was taking her time, slowly moving her body into the best position.

Paparella stood on his hind legs and frantically scratched at the side of the carrier. Beezel nodded to Mimi.

Mimi reached inside and grabbed the mouse. "If he doesn't behave," she told Gumdrop, "I'll give him right back. I promise."

Beezel pointed at the mouse. Ka-poof. Paparella was a mynah again.

"Ready to cooperate?" she asked him.

"What a horrible, horrible animal," Paparella squawked. "I've never liked snakes. If I can just point my claw at you"—Paparella tried to raise one bird foot off the ground—"you'll both be snake chow."

"You can't ka-poof someone once you're changed," Beezel said calmly. "Didn't you hear your mother say that? Or maybe she didn't get a chance to tell everything to Simon."

"You can't make me give it to you!" Paparella screeched. "You can't make me!"

"Well, let's think about that," Beezel said. "We've got you *and* all the time in the world. I think we'll just keep ka-poofing you and let you have lots of visits with Gumdrop."

"She'd love that," Mimi said. "Of course, Gumdrop can move very quickly when she wants to. Especially when she's really hungry. I might not always be able to get him out safely."

"No great loss there," huffed Hector. "She's welcome to him."

Paparella the mynah was quiet for a minute. "All right," he said. "I'll do it."

Beezel took the coin out of her pants pocket and held it between her thumb and index finger. She touched the coin to Paparella's bird claw. Mimi put her finger on the coin.

"Here goes," Beezel said to Mimi. She hoped the magic would flow back evenly between them, the way it was before. "Say the words," Beezel said to Paparella. "Now."

The Great Paparella said the magic words. The words that Beezel and Mimi had first heard spoken the night that Simon died.

When he was finished, Beezel put the coin back in her pocket. "Let's test it," she said to Mimi. "You go first."

Mimi pointed to Paparella. "NO!" he screeched.

Ka-poof. Paparella was a cockroach. Ka-poof. Paparella was the mynah bird.

"My half seems to be working just fine," Mimi said happily. "Try yours."

Beezel pointed to Paparella. "Not again!" he cawed. Ka-poof. Paparella was a slug. Ka-poof. Paparella was the mynah bird.

"We're back to normal!" Beezel said as she hugged Mimi.

"You'll be sorry," Paparella the mynah said to Beezel and Mimi. "I'll get my revenge, you'll see. I'll . . ."

"Oh, be quiet," Beezel said as she ka-poofed him into a toad and placed him back inside the backpack.

"Great job, girls," Mr. Whaffle said. "Now let's take this scoundrel to the police station and hand him over to Officer Dolton." He smiled at Beezel and Mimi as he started toward the door. "A full-size human Paparella, of course." He picked up Gumdrop's carrier and followed Hector out of the room.

Mimi grabbed Gadget's cage as she walked out the door. "Come on, Beezel," she called over her shoulder. "All this ka-poofing has made me hungry."

Beezel slipped on the backpack and started to follow them. She stopped. "Be right there!" she called after them. She took one last look at the room. "All out and over," she said softly. It was what Mr. Trimoni said each time a circus perform-ance was finished. She turned off the lights and closed the door behind her.

As they opened the stairwell door to the main floor, Beezel could see police lights flashing through the museum's windows. She heard a car door slam out-side and then a familiar voice.

"Oh no, it's Dolton!" Beezel turned and grabbed Mimi's arm. "Mimi, put Gadget down. We've got to change Paparella back before Officer Dolton gets in here."

Mimi put Gadget's cage on the reception desk. "Where should we do it?"

"Hector," Beezel said, "stall Officer Dolton for a minute. Then send him into the gift shop. Tell him we've got Paparella in there."

"Roger that," Hector said.

Mimi looked up at Mr. Whaffle. "Would you come with us, just in case he tries to escape?"

"Girls," Mr. Whaffle said as he set Gumdrop's carrier down, "it would be my pleasure."

Beezel, Mimi and Mr. Whaffle ran inside the gift shop.

"Over here!" Beezel said as she headed for a pile of life-size inflated aliens. "We'll ka-poof him back here!"

"Just one minute." Mr. Whaffle stopped in front of a table full of souvenirs. Picking up a concrete replica of a mummy, he swung it back and forth like a baseball bat. "This will stop him in his tracks if he tries to get away."

Beezel put the backpack down, took out Paparella and set him on the floor. She looked at Mimi. "Would you like to do the honors?" she said as she waved her hand toward Paparella the toad.

"Certainly!" Mimi pointed at the toad. Ka-poof. The Great Paparella looked down at them.

"I would stand very still if I were you," Mr. Whaffle said as he wielded his concrete mummy. "Nothing would make me happier than to bean you with this."

Paparella looked at their group, then stared at the inflated aliens that surrounded him. "What have you done *now*? What is this revolting place?" He pointed to the aliens. "And who are *they*?"

Officer Dolton burst into the gift shop. Following him were Hector and Professor Finkleroy, the owner of the museum.

"Are you girls okay?" Officer Dolton asked.

"Yes," the girls answered together.

Beezel pointed to Paparella. "There he is. He kidnapped my sister and strapped her into an electric chair."

Officer Dolton looked at Mimi.

"It's absolutely true," she said.

"Well, pal," Officer Dolton said as he unhooked a set of handcuffs from his belt. "We're going downtown. There are some people you need to talk to."

"But officer," Paparella said as he pointed to Beezel, "she took my magic coin, the little beast. And *then* she turned me into a mynah bird!" He shook his finger at Mimi. "But it was her snake that almost ate me!" Paparella pointed to Mr. Whaffle. "And *he* was some sort of nasty rodent!

He threw pens at me." He glared at Hector. "And that hideous little man was a mouse, and he *bit* me, right here on my finger!" He waved his finger in Officer Dolton's face. "I probably have rabies! I insist that you arrest all of them this minute!"

Officer Dolton glanced over at Beezel and Mimi and rolled his eyes. Beezel pointed to the side of her head and drew circles with her finger. As Officer Dolton locked the handcuffs on Paparella and led him out the door, he nodded to her in agreement.

"Well, you two girls have certainly had quite a day," Professor Finkleroy said. "Officer Dolton stopped by my house to see if I would let him search the museum for Paparella. So of course, I agreed." He scratched his head. "And this might not be the time or place, but as long as I have you both here . . ." He looked at Mr. Whaffle. "*And* your teacher . . . I wanted to make you an offer."

"An offer?" Beezel said.

"Yes," Professor Finkleroy said. "I was there on opening night and was quite impressed with your act. I'd like to make you an offer to perform in one of my hotels. I have hotels all over the world: Cairo, Bangkok, Paris, Rome."

"You *own* hotels?" Mimi said.

"Yes," Professor Finkleroy said. "I own not only the Museum of the Strange and Magical, but the Merlin Hotel chain as well."

"Well, I'll be a purple pachyderm," Hector said.

Beezel smiled at Mimi. She just might get to see all those cities after all. Then she had a thought. "Professor Finkleroy, you advertise who performs at your hotels, don't you?"

"Of course! It helps bring people into all my hotels *and* the museum."

"Well," Beezel said, suddenly shy. "Do you think you could mention that we're from the Trimoni Circus?"

"Why, certainly!" Professor Finkleroy patted her on the shoulder.

Mimi gave Beezel a hug. "You're brilliant," she said.

CHAPTER TWENTY

Mr. Whaffle finally found Mr. and Mrs. Trimoni. After hearing about Beezel and Mimi's adventures, their parents were all too happy to fly home a few days early.

The twins went with Mr. Whaffle and Hector to the airport. When Beezel and Mimi spotted their parents in the baggage claim area, they ran to meet them.

"Girls?" Mr. Trimoni said. "Are you okay?"

"We're fine, Dad," said Beezel as she hugged him. She thought she could smell circus popcorn on his old plaid jacket.

Mrs. Trimoni squeezed Beezel and Mimi. She didn't talk. She just clucked like a happy hen.

The twins told Mr. and Mrs. Trimoni all about

the missing coin. About the Great Paparella, Meredith, the Magic Duel and Mimi's kidnapping.

"That's my girls!" Mr. Trimoni said proudly. "Trimonis through and through. Always on their toes!"

"But it was Mr. Whaffle and Hector who saved our lives," said Beezel. She told her parents about the art pens and Hector's strong bite.

"You should have seen them," said Mimi.

"They were amazing," said Beezel.

Hector started crying when he saw his two best friends again.

"I've let you down," he said to Mrs. Trimoni. "All your nice things have been ruined."

"Nonsense," said Mrs. Trimoni. "Things are just *things*. They can be replaced." She hugged her daughters. "I have all my valuables right here. Safe and sound."

Mr. Whaffle got out his bandanna and wiped his eyes. "I think I'm getting a cold," he said.

Mr. Trimoni shook their hands. "I've got fine friends, fine friends," he said. He looked at Mr. Whaffle. "Correct me if I'm wrong, but are your teaching days over?"

Mr. Whaffle cleared his throat. "I think they are, yes," he said. "I'd like to give knife throwing another go. If you'll have me."

Mr. Trimoni slapped him on the back. "Wouldn't have it any other way. You know, Aqua Boy has truly missed performing with you."

Mr. Whaffle smiled proudly and straightened his goatee.

"Great!" said Beezel. "Does this mean we don't have to have a teacher?"

"No," said Mrs. Trimoni. "It means Hector will be your new teacher. If he wants to be, that is."

"I'll do my best," Hector said.

"Oh well," said Beezel. "If we *have* to have another teacher, I'm glad it's Hector."

Mr. Whaffle cleared his throat. "Now I have a surprise for you. And it's waiting for us at Merrill's Ice Cream Parlor."

Mr. Whaffle was very tight-lipped on the drive over to the ice cream parlor. He wouldn't answer any of their guesses as to what the surprise was. But the girls saw her as soon as they walked in the door. Meredith. She was his surprise.

"And we're engaged," said Meredith. "Again."
She laughed and told them Mr. Whaffle had called
her the day after Paparella was arrested.

"I wasn't going to make the same mistake twice,"
Mr. Whaffle said. He took her hand. "I think the
occasion calls for ice cream, and lots of it."

Mimi got a banana split with extra chocolate
syrup. "Can we have seconds?" she asked Mr. Whaffle.

"Thirds if you want," he said.

Beezel was eating her favorite dessert in the world:
a caramel sundae. As she scooped up a spoonful of
vanilla ice cream, she thought about Simon's
Changing Coin. It was wonderful to have it back.
They could do some pretty amazing tricks with
ka-poofing. And there were still two more coins out
there somewhere. The Shrinking Coin. And the
Mind-Reading Coin. She wondered if they'd ever find
out where they were. *I wish I had the Mind-Reading
Coin right now. I'd love to know what everyone is thinking.*

She looked across the table at her mom and dad.
They were laughing and whispering together.

She looked at Mimi. She had whipped cream in
her hair and chocolate syrup on her nose.

She looked at Hector. He had the hiccups. Mimi

was patting him on the back.

Mr. Whaffle carefully sipped a root-beer float. After each sip, he dabbed the corners of his mouth with a napkin. And sitting right next to him, drinking lemonade and holding his hand, was Meredith. They looked so happy.

"Well, girls," said Mr. Trimoni, "it would be hard to top this escapade. And I imagine you've had enough of the big city to last a lifetime."

Beezel looked at Mimi. Mimi looked at Beezel.

"I don't think so, Dad," Beezel said. "Performing in the city has been great."

"It's what *we* like to do on our vacation," said Mimi. "Just like what *you* like to do is discover new talent for the circus."

"Speaking of talent." Beezel kicked Mimi under the table. She grinned. "Did you catch a yeti?"

"What?" said Mr. Trimoni. "Who told you where we were? Why, if word got out—"

"Relax, Dad," said Mimi. "Beezel heard you talking before you left."

"So," said Beezel. "Did you bring him back? Will there be an Abominable Snowman in the Trimoni Circus?"

Mr. Trimoni shook his finger at her. "You can laugh if you want to, young lady," he said. "But let's just say this . . ." He took Mrs. Trimoni's hand and kissed it. "Your mother's charms won out in the end."

"Mom charmed a yeti?" said Mimi.

"You'll see," Mr. Trimoni smiled mysteriously. "But don't you two try to change the subject. I'm not sure I like you traipsing off to a new city every year while we're away on . . . business."

Mrs. Trimoni put her hand on top of her husband's. "It's what makes them happy, dear," she said. "Just like eating fire makes you happy."

Mr. Trimoni chuckled. "Or like swinging across the big top makes you happy," he said.

"Or throwing knives," said Mr. Whaffle.

"Or telling the future," said Meredith.

"Or taking care of my girls," said Hector.

"Or ka-poofing," said Mimi. "Right, Beez?"

"Yep," Beezel said. And there was one other thing that made her happy. Just as happy as cities and mysteries and magic.

She knew it when she saw Mimi smiling at her.